FRONTIER BRIDES

Will Kearny reckons he has a job for his working life, ramrodding iron-willed Peter Thwaites's Rocking T outfit, but after winning a bruising fight with the brutish troublemaker 'Bull' Jusserand, Kearny is dealt an inexplicable blow. Old Pete abruptly quits the struggle for survival and sells out to his sworn enemy – Jusserand's boss, the range-hog Franz Sturman. The mystery deepens when Sturman's lawyer traps Kearny into riding herd over a 'cargo of brides'. What is the secret of lovely Christine Smith, the sad-eyed, odd-girl-out among what proves to be a hell-raising bevy of fallen women?

FRONTIER BRIDES

FRONTIER BRIDES

by

Chap O'Keefe

Dales Large Print Books
Long Preston, North Yorkshire,
BD23 4ND, England.

British Library Cataloguing in Publication Data.

O'Keefe, Chap
    Frontier brides.

    A catalogue record of this book is
    available from the British Library

    ISBN   1-84262-409-1 pbk

First published in Great Britain 2004 by Robert Hale Limited

Published in Large Print 2005 by arrangement with
Robert Hale Ltd.

Dales Large Print is an imprint of Library Magna Books Ltd.

Printed and bound in Great Britain by
T.J. (International) Ltd., Cornwall, PL28 8RW

1

DANCING TO DEATH

She looked to be in her late twenties. Unpinned, her long hair swirled freely in response to every vigorous movement. She was gaudy in a yellow peasant blouse and a red satin skirt.

'Dance, Nita, dance!' chanted the sweaty-faced circle of male spectators mostly in dowdy Levi work pants and collarless shirts. She whirled and twirled to the frenzied scraping of Dr Holdstock's fiddle. Her legs kicked higher, showing frilly petticoats and glimpses of more than ankle. Passing towns-women pursed their lips. They tightened their grips on market baskets and turned flushing faces away in unconcealed disgust.

But Nita's fluid dance steps and alluring body were what interested Franz Sturman more than ordinarily in what was going on around the painted wagon drawn up between the bank and the First Claim Saloon on the main drag of Rawhide Fork.

The prim townswomen's disapproval was equalled in degree by the rich cattleman's excitement.

Sturman saw that signwriting in ornate script on the wagon's body garishly advertised 'Dr Holdstock's Travelling Medicine Show'. Dr Holdstock was fiftyish, a beanpole wearing a thick wool Prince Albert and tight striped trousers despite the heat of the day. But the eyes of the swelling crowd – and Sturman's – were all glued on his help, Nita.

A scruffy boy of about eleven contrived to trip over his older brother's big work boots and rolled in the dust right at the dancing girl's feet. His brother grabbed his shirt top and yanked him clear of the lifting skirt. The smaller boy's voice was shrill and unbroken. 'I seen it! I seen it! She's got no drawers on.'

The crowd hooted. The big brother blushed. He bunched the boy's shirt in his fist, choking off further indiscretions, cuffed him and dragged him away.

Sturman had two insatiable appetites: one was for rangeland – they called it 'grass' in the Territory of New Mexico in the 1880s – and the other was for ladies of the night. With the aid of his Arrowhead crew of gun-handy ruffians, the cattleman could help himself to vast tracts of grass, dispossessing former claimants with ruthless ease. But with women he was faced with a more challenging problem of supply.

On this part of the frontier there were your Mexicans and 'breeds, of course, but the few wholly white American females – even the whores – were quickly married off to the males outnumbering them. And once married, a punishing climate and wifely duties to husbands scrabbling primitive livings off a cruel land quickly reduced most of them to unattractive drudges: lank hair, lined faces, calloused hands and sagging figures in sun-faded and patched calico.

Sturman feasted his eyes on Nita's provocative assets. A handsome piece, this quack medico's assistant, doing fine at drawing the ranch-town's suckers to his wagon where after the show was over he'd unload his dubious elixirs and unguents for their dollars. Maybe that night the woman would be required to lie with some of Dr Holdstock's very best customers in the bed of the painted wagon. The thought irritated Sturman and he decided there and then to possess this Nita solely for himself. Until he tired of her, that was.

Accordingly, Sturman later treated Dr Holdstock to a generous supper in a private room at the First Claim. The man ungratefully rejected his overtures, especially the proposal that he should pass over his employee into Sturman's service. 'No, no – out of the question, sir,' he said, greedily mopping the very last scrap of gravy from his plate with a crust of white bread. 'Miss Nita is – uh – indentured to my good self.'

'Well, we'll wrastle all that out later. My attorney in town here, Mr Seabury Reece, could draw up a very advantageous certificate of transfer, I'm sure,' Sturman said, thinking to play the game. But Dr Holdstock was adamant in his refusal.

Thereby he sealed his fate.

When Dr Holdstock's wagon headed out of Rawhide Fork next day, an ambush was arranged. On a treacherous stretch of the stage road, where to one side the ground fell away dizzyingly into a canyon, four armed Arrowhead toughs rode out from behind a rocky outcropping. They brought the wagon to a halt and ordered Dr Holdstock's pretty woman to get down.

The quack protested. He was swiftly clubbed to death with the stock of a shotgun. Then his corpse, the wagon and its two squealing horses were pitched into the canyon so it would appear an unfortunate accident had taken place.

The evidence of foul play tumbled end over end to the rocks far below. The wagon was smashed to splintery bits.

Nita, screaming, was thrown across the back of an unmounted horse the Arrowhead bunch had brought with them for the purpose. Her wrists and ankles were bound tight with rope and linked under the horse's belly.

Then she was led off to Franz Sturman's *hacienda* at his Arrowhead ranch head-quarters.

The cattleman was a big man of forty or so, who carried some spare fat but not much and had a sleek presence that told no lies when it spoke of power and money. A brown frock coat was hitched back behind the ivory handles of a pair of matched Colt .45s slung from a wide gunbelt that with a wine-coloured, saffron-embroidered vest partly concealed the beginnings of a paunch.

Alone with her, Sturman told Nita her days of dancing and whoring for a living were over. She could live in comfort under his care and protection. 'Sure, you're here for my pleasure. There'll be some demands, but a spunky, travelled gal knows about them.'

But Nita shrank back, repulsed. 'No! I don't want anything to do with you, you murderer. Let me go!'

Do what he would, Sturman found it impossible to force her. Finally, he said, 'Right, you slut! You'll suffer for this. I'll give you to my crew. When they've done working you over, you'll be apt to do as you're told!'

Sturman hollered and Nita was removed to a barn by his drooling hardcases.

They were well liquored-up with the redeye whiskey the boss had given them as a bonus for the elimination of Dr Holdstock. Free licence to do as they willed with this pretty young woman brought an unexpected excitement to their celebration.

'I got a mind to see the med'cine man's dancin' gal dance *nekkid!*' one of them said. Louis Jusserand was gross: a mountain of a man, a giant they called 'Bull'. He had a wide, flat face. Any expression on it had to compete with the dominating ugliness of a flat, hair-sprouting nose and black eyes that were narrow and cruel. When he laughed, his lips parted over jagged, dirty teeth.

Jusserand's sidekicks roared approval. An accordion was produced. Nita was compelled to strip to the 'music' squeezed out of it by a bald-headed tobacco chewer. Persuasion was

12

applied in the form of a dog whip, produced by Bull Jusserand. It had a wooden handle and a single strand of leather, quite thick and heavy, which he cracked at her ankles, making her jump.

'Stop! Stop! I'll dance,' she pleaded. 'I'll do anything!'

She danced for them till they tired of watching her and she was ready to drop. Then those who weren't too drunk pressed further unwanted attentions on her. They worked together like ropers and iron-handlers at roundup time. She put up a frenzied fight, wriggling with superhuman strength. Her screams and her punishers' curses could be heard by Sturman back in the house, where he gloated on the girl's terror.

But Nita finally recognized the futility of struggle. She accepted the inevitable, and almost to the end, thought she'd been spared the worst horror: the monstrous, big-bellied Bull Jusserand. His huge girth made satisfying his desires difficult. So it was agreed he'd take her last. He pushed her off a stack of hay bales to the hard-packed dirt floor.

'God, no!' she gasped. She scrambled, sobbing, onto hands and knees. It was then that Jusserand pushed her shoulders down with a mighty shove so that one cheek of her turned face struck the abrasive dirt. His great, 300 pound weight pushed down on her from behind and Nita's braced legs trembled.

'Get him off me!' she cried. 'He's too much! *He'll kill me!*'

But no one was fit to hear the panic in her yells. Drunkenness and exhaustion had taken hold.

Her legs buckled. Jusserand collapsed, grunting hoarsely, inarticulate and insensible to the havoc he was wreaking. Possibly he ruptured her kidneys; possibly a smashed rib penetrated a lung, suffocating her with her own blood. Whatever, Nita's fear was realized. When he didn't lift or roll off, she was killed by the crushing dead weight of Jusserand's repletion.

Afterward, Franz Sturman was galled by the sudden loss of his potential new plaything, but he had a surprising tolerance of Bull Jusserand's crimes, like an indulgent master with a pet dog inclined to forget its training.

Sturman mused on Nita's death, seeking to see what could be learned or how it might be turned to advantage. His conclusion was that Rawhide Fork needed more women.

Why, the one-horse burg couldn't boast a single whorehouse! The place needed a supply of women more willing than Nita. They could entertain him; they could be used to reward members of his crew.

He pondered for several days just how it could be achieved before hitting on a brilliant scheme. The beauty of it was it would cost him nothing and would help achieve another of his land-grabbing goals at the same time.

Beyond a humped ridge, the best acres of Rocking T range lay shimmering and deserted – an undulating patchwork of brown and green. The land was undotted by beast or man like the sweep of blue sky overhead was unbroken by cloud.

Will Kearny, an able and shrewd foreman to his last tough inch, gazed on the sweeping emptiness. A brow-lowering frown darkened features gaunted and already deeply tanned by New Mexican sun and wind.

Cattle were absent even from the swale at the foot of the ridge. Ordinarily a bunch of Rocking T cows and calves congregated there, chomping complacently. Spring water seeped up in the bottom, even in the driest summer, and the blue-spiked grama grass was made brilliant by wildflowers.

The missing stock spelled trouble.

Not that Kearny and trouble were strangers. He'd seen plenty, way back. Orphaned on the frontier as a stripling of eleven, young Will had grown up fast, learning how you fought and survived in the hard school called life. Before age seventeen, he'd had several surprised and dead bullies down his back-trail. He'd also ridden on a cattle drive to Dodge City, Kansas, clashing with Kiowas and rustlers all the bloody way.

Kearny and the rider with him reined up atop the low ridge. The sun beat heavily upon them. 'Empty!' the rider said. 'An' yuh c'n bet where they'll be.'

Sitting his saddle, Kearny pushed back his hat. He scratched his head. Black hair, cropped short, had already begun to grey at the temples though Kearny was still young, short of thirty.

'Reckon so. Unless we really have got us a case of rustlers this time, the critters'll be in the chaparral.'

The Rocking T was in rolling country on the verge of being rough. But good grazing was to be had. Contented beeves had no reason to stray into the thick tangle of brush situated on its northern fringe. Elsewhere, when the pasture gave way, it was to near-arid, scrub-strewn slopes where grey clumps of sagebrush dominated, seldom more than two to four feet tall. That was benign growth compared to the brush.

Kearny didn't relish having to drive the missing cows out of the chaparral. The animals should've been reluctant to enter it. Yet the longer they were left, the harder it would be to prise them out. Fearing the scent of horse and man, they would crash deeper into the brushy thickets. Imprisoned or liberated in the dense maze, they would bawl complaint, grow wilder each day.

'Damn and blast it!' Kearny said, his weariness evaporated by the fire of anger. 'It ain't as if this is the first time, Arch. I'm getting sick of these fool stunts, and I suspicion who's back of them.'

Two dozen mean plant species augmented the chaparral in a variety of combinations. Towering prickly pear and low-growing cat-claw with vicious thorns could snag the hoofs of cattle or horses like fish-hooks. Sweat, dust and curses would be raised before men and beasts emerged from the punishing gather, bleeding from innumerable cuts and nicks, if nothing worse.

They rode down into the swale.

Arch Leggat, a rawhide knot of a cow-hand, stroked his bristly chin with a work-gnarled hand. He wasn't a fast thinker, but when he considered something, Kearny knew he'd duly come up with the right, practical answer.

Leggat swore softly. He pointed to the tracks that marked the stock's exit. 'They bin driven north sure 'nough, Will. There's horse prints clear in the softer earth two riders gathered several dozen head, I'd say.'

The Rocking T pair took out in pursuit.

'Damn them! Damn....' Kearny said. 'But maybe this time we'll put an end to their games. Look, the sign's fresh. That dung's been dropped not past an hour. The sun's scarce crusted it.'

They galloped apace across the hills and hollows that were the brand's graze, their horses' manes and tails whipped in the wind of their making.

Less than a half-hour's hard riding was behind them when, through the dancing heat haze, a lift of dust came into sight. They restrained their mounts' headlong rush and a far-off sound drifted back to them. It was the bawling of cattle – the protest they might raise when being forced where they didn't want to go.

18

Kearny swung his chestnut's head. He put it into a short run up the steep slope to one side. The surefooted cow-country bronc picked its own path to the rim of the higher ground. Then Kearny twisted in creaking leather to tug from his saddle-bag an old pair of army field glasses. He held them to his eyes and focused.

'I guessed it right, Arch!' His look was smouldering as he lowered the glasses. Leggat's figuring was right, too. A pair of waddies was chousing a small herd of balky cows toward the hated chaparral. And they were Rocking T stock. With the powerful glasses he could clearly make out the brands on their left flanks.

Kearny rejoined his pard, glowering. His knuckles showed white as he gripped the reins, holding in his anger. 'The bastards are Arrowhead men,' he said.

'Yuh sure?'

'One of 'em was Bull Jusserand.'

'Uh-huh,' Leggat grunted. 'Thar's no mistakin' the big Frenchie. He's a mighty bad cuss to cross.'

Kearny didn't try to correct the bit Leggat had wrong: Louis Jusserand was of very mixed blood. Built big as a barn, and with a hint of Indian, he'd been born in America of parentage less certain than that his handle had been carried across the Plains from Louisiana to Santa Fe by French traders in the last century.

'Some men are born to troublemaking,' Kearny said. 'Jusserand is dangerous not just because he's vicious and stupid and has the shoulder width and strength of two ordinary men, but also because he's at Franz Sturman's beck and call like a dog to its master.'

'Yeah, if Bull Jusserand's back of the low-down tricks played on the Rocking T – tearin' down fences, burnin' hay, spookin' beeves an' such – yuh can bet it's on Mr High-an'-Mighty Sturman's orders.'

Jusserand and Franz Sturman were a daunting combination to go up against. Sturman laid claim to most of the basin. His vast holdings' fertile acres, adjoining the Rocking T, were the best in the county. He was a powerful and ambitious operator. Plenty had learned to their cost it was best not to stand in his way.

But Kearny knew he had to force this business to a showdown.

'If we turn a blind eye to what we now know is happening, Arch, Arrowhead is gonna keep right on riding roughshod all over Rocking T till Pete Thwaites agrees to sell out to Sturman.'

'The old man'd never do that. He's got no place else to go an' we fellers in his crew would all be outa jobs.'

Kearny's expression grew grimmer. 'Pete's struggling, Arch, and there's few of us left. No matter how tightly I ramrod the spread, he can't keep on taking losses. But I reckon you're right. Pete would rather be carried off the Rocking T feet-first than slope out with Sturman's *dinero.*'

'Hell, the way yuh put it, I guess we ain't got no choice, Will ... we gotta stop them cows bein' driven off. I hope we can do it peaceable.'

Doubt tinged Leggat's last words. Kearny shrugged. 'Let's stop palavering and go find out.'

2

FISTS, BOOTS AND EDUCATION

The Rocking T pair were canny. They chose a spot dotted with brush where chances were less that they would be seen, moving in on the Arrowhead riders and the bunch of uneasy cattle from opposite sides.

Jusserand and his companion were having a hard time of it. The cows were fractious. The beasts milled about them so they had to give most of their attention to cursing and kicking at them to keep them hazed in the general direction of the chapparal.

They stopped their work when they saw Kearny and Leggat and sat their horses waiting. Jusserand's sidekick, a greasy puncher called Baldy for reasons obvious whenever he doffed his sweat-stained hat, tried not to look like a kid caught with his fingers in the cookie jar. He produced a plug of tobacco and bit out a big chunk with affected nonchalance.

Kearny nudged his mount alongside Jusserand's. 'These are Rocking T beeves.' He nodded his head at the nearest cow's flank. 'Can't you read brands, Mr Jusserand?'

'Sure, Kearny. That's why we're movin' 'em. They'd – uh – strayed onto our graze.'

Kearny shook his head. 'Try again. We cut your sign in a swale well inside Rocking T boundary lines. This time the tracks are fresh and clear.'

Jusserand's slow wits visibly digested this. His massive jaw tightened. 'What do yuh mean? Yuh callin' me a liar?'

Kearny suspected Jusserand's indignation sprang mostly from someone having the temerity to question what he cared to tell him. It had to be a novel experience for the notorious bully.

Baldy spat a stream of brown juice after the retreating cows, wiped his mouth with the back of his hand.

Leggat muttered under his breath. Kearny caught the word 'careful'. It wasn't hard to get the drift of his warning. Push Jusserand too far and he would be apt to go crazy wild. Both men had seen Jusserand toss 250 pound kegs into a wagon like they weighed a hundred. With his dander up, his strength equalled that of six normal men.

Kearny was no milksop. He had a heap of experience in handing bunkhouse rebels their comeuppance. Rancher Thwaites had faith in his capacity for facing down trouble. The men respected him. He had a reputation for rough honesty, was quick-fisted and chain-lightning with a Colt. Not one ordinary cow-hand within a hundred miles would choose to tangle with him.

But Jusserand was something else.

Leggat swallowed, and waited and watched.

Kearny looked Jusserand straight back in the eye. 'For a man with more muscle than brain, you're doing well,' he said drily. If Jusserand was antagonized, so be it. It was time to force this thing to a head.

'And you can go tell your lord and master Mr Franz Sturman that the Rocking T ain't standing for any more of your messing with its property.'

Kearny was able to put in this extra advice while his previous insult was still percolating through Jusserand's thick skull.

The message may not have gotten through before Jusserand barged his mount into the side of Kearny's chestnut. With a roar of animal rage, the man-mountain lunged out of the saddle, launching his considerable weight at Kearny.

If Kearny had not been ready for him, the

chestnut's legs would have surely buckled. But Kearny was sidestepping his bronc and kicking his feet free of the stirrups.

Jusserand's horse trumpeted shrilly. Jusserand wrapped one ham-like arm round Kearny's neck and flailed wildly with the other. Kearny let himself go limp. He slid from the saddle.

The two men crashed to the widening patch of dirt between the horses' dancing hoofs. For a moment, Kearny was pinned under Jusserand's thrashing bulk. But the big man was winded by the heavy fall, his armlock broken. And Kearny, despite being bruised and numbed, had neither heard nor felt any crack of bones.

Jusserand lurched up onto his knees, swinging his huge arms and fists with fury though little direction and no skill. Kearny put his efforts into rolling clear and scrambling to his feet.

One of Jusserand's brute blows happened to glance across Kearny's face, smashing lips and bringing a spurt of blood into his mouth as his teeth carved into the inside of his cheek. Then he was free and standing.

Jusserand hauled himself onto his legs with another wordless roar. Kearny shaped up to meet his next attack.

Baldy spat again. 'Keep hittin' him, Bull! Clobber him *harder!* Make him *bleed!*'

Jusserand rushed in for what he thought would be the kill. The lumbering charge was suggestive of the animal that gave him his nickname.

Kearny knew no man could take much of the punishment Jusserand handed out by reason of sheer bulk and power. Give or take some – but not much – Jusserand turned the scales at 300 pounds. Kearny dodged away.

'He's yeller!' Baldy crowed, ejecting a spray of more brown spittle. 'Ain't got the spunk to hit back!'

Every man in the county knew Jusserand's fighting style was all dirty, without science and effective because of his size, reach and weight. Punch him and it had the effective-ness of a fleabite. The Arrowhead crew had many times exulted over Jusserand's demo-lition of unwary strangers who'd given them offence in the saloon and streets of Rawhide Fork. Invariably, his methods included head-butting, eye-gouging, rabbit-punching and stomping.

So each time the giant drove at him, Kearny slipped aside, knowing it was disaster if Jusserand's clutching hands hauled him into a bear-crushing clinch.

He also got in some quick, arm-jarring blows of his own: to the side of Jusserand's jaw, to his ear, to his biceps. It was like punching a sack of damp sand. Jusserand had some fat, but not much. He was mostly solid muscle on a frame of big bones. He just absorbed the punches.

Jusserand finally figured he wasn't achieving a whole lot outside of starting to sound like a blown horse and making a spectacle of himself while the nimble-footed Kearny ducked, wheeled and hopped. With a bellow of outrage he suddenly pulled up.

Kearny instantly darted in to crunch his knuckles more or less ineffectively into the Neanderthal jaw.

'Suckered!' Jusserand grunted – and swung his hard-capped boot into Kearny's abdomen as he sprang away.

Kearny doubled over, retching, and Jusserand slapped him on down like he was swatting a fly. Kearny writhed on the ground, gagging for breath and dazed. Jusserand kicked at his helpless form, rolling him over onto his back.

Through his befuddlement, Kearny got a flash picture of what the cruel giant had in his dirty mind. He was going to stomp on his pain-racked belly, using his spur rowels to slash the multiple layers of taut muscle, causing them to come apart. A man thus gutted was good as doomed. His bladder would swell out and rupture. The result was agony, death.

All the time Kearny had left was the fractional respite customary before Jusserand put thought into action.

Kearny summoned his last reserves to ignore the hundred centres of pain that spiked his battered body; he flung himself aside.

Jusserand jumped on the spot he'd cleared. His boots raised a cloud of dust. He tottered off balance, bewildered by Kearny's speedy avoidance of the kill.

Kearny gave himself no mercy. There was not likely to be a second chance. He threw himself back in a tackle. His shoulder thudded into his swaying foe's legs behind the knees.

Jusserand crashed over like a gigantic ponderosa pine felled by the lumberjack's axe. Unluckily for him, his head struck a boulder with a dull, sickening thud. But still he hauled himself stupefied onto hands and knees, shaking his head like a stunned ox. Even the scary craftiness had left his eyes; they were glassy, empty of all intelligence.

Kearny forced himself upright, though his

legs felt like he was drunk. He had to finish this. He unshucked his Colt, stepped up and belted the dazed tough behind the ear with the barrel.

Jusserand at last keeled over into total insensibility.

Baldy looked as though he might choke on his chaw. 'Goddamnit,' he said in an awed voice. 'Yuh put him out cold!'

'He started it,' Kearny told him, through thick and bloody lips. 'Consider it for his education.'

'Sonofabitch! Yuh could of busted his head.'

'I know Bull Jusserand's head. No gun iron is going to break it. Get yourself and your pard off this grass as soon as and any way you can. You stay away from the Rocking T from here on out, or there'll be bigger trouble. You hear?'

Arch Leggat could hardly believe the outcome: Bull Jusserand whupped and Baldy Hogsden too shocked to give lip!

But Jusserand was going to have more than a headache; he was going to have a grudge. And Leggat had an uneasy feeling bigger problems were around the corner for Kearny.

'The big bastard will be doubly dangerous

now, Will,' he warned quietly. 'He ain't liable to take this lyin' down.'

'Let him take it howsoever he likes!'

3

GIRL IN DEBT

On a bright summer morning in New York City, Christine Smith opened her door to a knock. The rooms in which she lived and worked were above a grocery store in a quarter several blocks removed from the moneyed broad avenues and hotels at the bustling city's hub. It was not Hell's Kitchen but what a kind observer might call shabby genteel.

The knocker was the proprietor of the store, her landlord, Eli Greenbaum. Christine knew it from the peculiarly shuffling footsteps that had preceded the three rapid taps on the door's thin wooden panel. The sinking feeling she felt in her stomach was only partly related to the increasing inadequacy of her diet.

'Good day to you, Mr Greenbaum,' she said. She tried to put a smile on her face to match the brightness outside the muslin-curtained windows of her mean surroundings.

Greenbaum was a wizened, one-time immigrant with a bushy black beard and darkly fixing sparrow's eyes. His acknowledgment was gruff and he got right down to business, as was his way.

'Good morning, Miss Smith. Your rent is now four weeks overdue. I have to be paid.'

His tone was harsh and abrupt and to her irritation the ultimatum made Christine flinch, like an inexperienced cab horse to the cut of the whip.

She admonished herself silently. Like her mother before her − a stickler for correct manners − she was being too refined, too sensitive for this place. Mr Greenbaum's hard mouth slitted in a smile. Satisfaction at her discomfiture? Calculation?

The thought was not new. Greenbaum had an uncanny knack for being able to turn others' misfortune to his personal profit. Behind his back in his grocery store, she'd heard him described as a bloodsucking rogue. Perhaps it was the explanation of his strides in the New World where others such as her mother had only stumbled.

Christine went cold inside. She had a sudden premonition that today the time had finally come ripe for Greenbaum to speak what was on his mind. To make demands.

But that was silly. She must put a halter on imagination. Beyond overdue rent, there was nothing this grasping man of business would want to ask of her.

In the eye of her beholder, Miss Christine Smith was a comely maiden, blessed with a milk-hued, smooth young complexion most fetching when tinted with a rose-pink blush as it was now. Grave, violet-blue eyes gave an appealing vulnerability to her open countenance. She groomed herself with care and her most notable characteristic was a full crown of brushed-out, dark hair. It formed a great, frizzy halo around her head in a shaft of the dust-laden sunlight.

Her liquid eyes took on an added glistening under Greenbaum's assessing stare. 'Oh, dear,' she said. 'Since poor Mama passed away, it has been so difficult.'

She turned from him into her living quarters which were dominated by two sewing machines. They were of the drophead type and one of them was being used as a table. It was covered with a lacy cloth, so only the curved framework of the iron stand and treadle could be seen.

The tablecloth was a shroud to shared endeavour.

'Providence has not been kind to me, Mr

Greenbaum,' Christine said. 'With the pair of us sewing, we could just afford to scrape by in New York. Mama was so much better as a machinist than I.'

'Tchah!' Greenbaum said. 'Your mother coddled you.' He scratched his beak of a nose, reflecting. 'Are you sure she left you no savings, no little nest-egg? What about your father?'

Christine sighed at his eager prompting; he had no idea.

'Mama was – alienated. That is, she left her husband when I was age ten. He'd brought her to live in a drab cow town in New Mexico. The frontier life was unbearably dreary to her and she finally abandoned him and returned East with me so that we might associate with people of quality. I've no money and no foreseeable means of getting any. At Mama's graveside, I realized I was completely by myself for the first time in my life. Truly alone.'

Greenbaum grunted. 'Then perhaps you should go West and look for your father, so I can rent out my rooms to someone else.'

'The thought has naturally occurred to me, Mr Greenbaum. But how can I make such a journey without money to pay for tickets and accommodation?'

The dumpy grocer-landlord lifted his shoulders. 'Is your problem, my dear... First and above all, you *must* pay me what you owe.'

Christine felt the beginnings of panic. Clearly, she had driven Greenbaum to the limits of his patience. She gulped. 'The few coins I have in my purse will scarcely buy necessities to see me through the week. I'll pay you as soon as I can, Mr Greenbaum.'

'That's always what you say, but good intentions can no longer suffice. It's not fitting that you should live on my charity.'

'I understand that. But what can I do?'

'You must work!' he said, putting a snap into his words.

'I do, yet even when I labour long hours the money's never enough to meet my expenses.'

Greenbaum nodded to himself with what seemed to Christine like a grim kind of satisfaction. 'So! This sewing is perhaps not for you. You will do other kinds of work, yes?'

Christine frowned. 'I know no other work.'

'But you have your natural talents. Like other young women in your reduced circumstances you must learn to use them. The world owes none of us a living, my dear.'

Greenbaum crooked a pudgy finger and beckoned her out onto the landing, where a dusty window overlooked the street. 'Let us quit avoiding the issue. Do you see that girl set at the corner?'

'That newspaper seller? Of course.'

'She's not more than sixteen years old but she has done her growing up. She rents a room much smaller than yours in one of the tenements I own in a different part of town. She always pays me on time. Nor does she starve to do it.'

'Do you suggest that I should sell newspapers or shift to humbler lodgings?'

Greenbaum fixed her with his beady eyes. 'Neither. I merely suggest it's time you earned your keep and freed yourself from the high-and-mighty notion you are something better than that newspaper seller or her sisters.'

Christine was not a worldly person, yet nor was she naïve. She'd lived in New York for nine years and knew that many of the girls in the city's legion of newspaper and flower sellers made ends meet by offering their favours to the men they met on the street. She had sometimes overheard them soliciting with their wheedling opening line, 'Give me a penny, mister?'

An angry retort sprang to her quivering lips. She was a well-brought-up young lady. Even casual smiles to strangers were not permitted in polite society. Just in time she bit the words back.

'What is it you want of me, Mr Greenbaum?' she asked instead, her voice wobbling.

'I want to help you earn your rent,' he said. Sensing she'd understood him, he schooled the harshness from his voice and made it a purr. 'I can arrange for you to meet a gentleman who would be happy to pay far more than for the services of a common newspaper seller who, I hear, doesn't even have a regular bath. It can be done very privately. Just like your good self, no one would want it any other way.'

The prospect of going with a strange man for money appalled Christine. Greenbaum had no business putting such a proposition to her. She'd always been a good girl. She *was* a good girl. But she let the instant for indignation pass. Her ongoing situation was precarious.

'I – I must have time to make a decision,' she faltered.

She'd always known the little grocer's commercial operations ranged far and wide.

She might even have had suspicions they included trade in pleasures of the flesh. But that he'd harboured intentions to snare her – the daughter of his deceased tenant – into these toils hadn't crossed her mind. How ingenuous she'd been!

Greenbaum nodded firmly several times before he turned to take the stairs.

'Yes, Miss Smith. You think about it. But not for too long. Not for too long.'

In fact it took just two days. When the hansom cab Eli Greenbaum summoned arrived in front of the store, he called Christine down from her room and unlocked the cashbox he kept under his counter. He counted out coins begrudgingly and handed them to her.

'The cabman, like yourself, has his directions and knows where to go. Pay him two dollars. These cabmen are regular highwaymen, and he may wish to charge more, but under no circumstances must you do so. The other two dollars will bring you back.'

Deep down, Christine's instincts pleaded against the coming ordeal. Her thoughts on the matter had ranged from terror to tearful self-pity. But impelled by the hopeless bind in which she found herself, she believed 'false pride and emotion' had been overcome. All that was left was a longing that the deed could already be over and done with.

She'd reasoned that her other immediate option was to flee the protection of Greenbaum's roof, abandoning what livelihood and scanty possessions she still had to become a New York beggar.

Maybe she could eventually enter the service of some wealthy family, but such positions were hard come by and she'd no experience of waged domestic work. More likely she would stay on the streets, just another among the teeming city riff-raff. Without lodgings or protection, the outcome of that course would be even blacker and more certain than what was now arranged for her. There wasn't a day when gossip didn't have it that several streetwalkers from among the big city's half-million inhabitants had been found dead from disease, foul play or self-poisoning.

Her initial shock at Greenbaum's proposition, she'd rationalized, went to show how little she really knew – about life and men and herself.

Greenbaum let his sharp gaze travel over her from head to toe. She'd put on her best dress, a long-sleeved purple calico with white polka dots. It was a showpiece of her seamstress's skills, trimmed with white ruffles at the neck and cuffs. The close-fitting bodice buttoned down the front. No skirt hoops, no underthings reliant on whalebones and laces, Greenbaum had said. 'But of course – ahem – it's plain your dainty figure has no recourse to artifice.'

Ready to leave, Christine felt that Greenbaum's greedy eyes were unpicking every stitch of the dress. The result evidently pleased him. His hands rasped as he rubbed them together.

'Very pretty, very pretty,' he said. 'You must readily yield to the gentleman every privilege he might demand. Remember, he has paid me your rent and your debt is to him. Indeed, I've put myself to much trouble and pledged my own word he'll not be disappointed.'

Christine didn't know how to answer. His look brought a heat to her cheeks, and a strange turmoil within. Dry-mouthed, she stood shifting her slight weight nervously from one foot to the other. Outside, the impatient cab driver was climbing down from his box.

'Well, get along, girl, get along!' Greenbaum said. 'The cabman knows the house.

Don't forget – you go up two flights, along the passage, first door on the right. All will be well. It's nothing a healthy young woman cannot do; nothing that will be hard.'

'I wish I could feel as sure as you do,' Christine blurted, gathered her skirt and rushed out.

The cab carried her through streets that grew increasingly narrow and shabby. Ten minutes later it arrived before a run-down tenement near the waterfront.

'This is the place, ma'am,' the cabman said. Contrary to Greenbaum's expectation, he took his fare without argument, but he shook his head wonderingly. 'Never before brought the likes of a lady like you here,' he said. 'But I guess it ain't any o' my business.'

'Exactly,' Christine said, and turned quickly to mount the building's porch steps, secretly scared that if the conversation was pursued she might lose what little courage she had and change her mind.

The cabman took his whip from the bracket and wheeled away. Christine pushed open a door that long ago had been given a coat of red paint now faded and peeling.

Inside, a tiny lobby was filled with a trash barrel and a pungent smell of urine, vomit and decay. She imagined the place was used as a night-time resort by down-and-out drunks. She suppressed a shudder, held her breath, and pressed on up a flight of rickety stairs, dark and no wider than two shoulder widths.

The first door on the right in the passage at the head of the second flight of stairs was ajar. It swung open when she put her hand to the tarnished brass doorknob.

A man was behind it.

'Come right on in, little darling,' he said. He stepped back and motioned her through, so that she saw the room first.

It was a cramped, dim place with only one soot-stained window that looked out to the blank brick wall of another building less than five feet away. The room had just one chair. Draped over it was a man's suit coat, a cravat and a small pistol in a harness. There was also a dresser and in the centre a double bed with an off-white, fleecy cover that had been well rumpled since it had last seen a smoothing iron.

The spotted oval mirror above the dresser reflected a lissome girl with a slightly heaving bosom and wide eyes in a pale, scared face under a spread umbrella of hair. Herself.

Panic seized her. She whirled on her heel

to leave, but a strong hand clamped long, vice-like fingers round her wrist. 'Uh-uh, no backing out, dearie! Mr Eli warned me you might be a little shy.'

The man jerked her into the room and turned a key in the door lock. He then withdrew the key and pushed it into the pocket of his striped trousers.

He was in his middle years – long-legged, barrel-chested, but still robust and straight-backed with his belly flat under his belt. An older woman, in a public situation where she was not disadvantaged, might have found in him a roguish attractiveness. His complexion was inclined to blotchiness, however, and his puffy nose was red-veined above a waxed grey moustache. He wore a yellow shirt with a separate celluloid collar under an unbuttoned, rosebud-embroidered vest. His thinning hair was smarmed down with pomade.

He also smelled of cigar smoke and liquor was on his breath.

A dissolute man about town, was the thought that came to Christine. She was frightened.

'I – I'm sorry,' she stammered. 'I've changed my mind.'

The man smirked. 'You *are* an innocent, aren't you? Well, I'm a retired officer and a gentleman, and there's nothing to be afeared of, missy. You know the deal. Your debts will be wiped off the slate easy. Once you've done it the first time, you'll think nothing of it. A pretty woman like you is made for a man to enjoy.'

Tears glistened her eyes. 'I can't! Lying with a stranger would be loathsome. It – it's not in my morality.'

The puffy face responded to her distress with an impatient grimace. The man spoke more curtly.

'Prudish, eh? Fact is, the pleasure of unburdening you of your modesty has already been sold to me anyway, so you might as well make up your mind to want the experience.'

'I won't. Never!'

'Fight me and I declare it'll be twice as bad for you. I don't appreciate stand-offishness. Nor being crossed.'

The man's uncompromising tone confirmed in Christine's mind that he was a monster. She pushed at his chest with a free hand and wrenched her other wrist out of his clammy grasp. She rattled furiously at the knob of the locked door.

'Let me out! Help!'

The man laughed scornfully but made no

attempt to restrain her. 'Lordy, if you were to scream your head off, no one in this neighbourhood would take notice! So you might as well save your breath.'

He went to the single window and pushed it up to call down into the alley below. 'Coote!'

'Somethin' wrong, sir?'

'Looks like I may need your help in acquainting Greenbaum's tenant with her duties, Sergeant. Come on up, will you?'

A ribald cackle drifted up. 'Only too glad, Major – long as thar's a bounty.'

Christine accepted the locked door wasn't going to budge. The window slid down with a screech and a thump. She pleaded, trying to stop her voice from shaking.

'Sir, will you please let me leave? I'll tell Mr Greenbaum to return your money.'

The discharged major scoffed. 'Like hell he will. Besides, because of your hemming and hawing, we now have Sergeant Coote to square as well.'

Footsteps thumped on the bare planks of the landing outside. The major advanced in a couple of strides, seized her round her slim waist and swept her aside. She stumbled backwards, her legs tangling with her skirt till they collided with the bed and she collapsed onto its lumpy surface. Much-abused springs screeched.

The major unlocked the door to let in his man.

The former sergeant wasn't the dandy his master was. He was dressed in a sweat-stained olive-green shirt and baggy grey pants held up by suspenders. A bit shorter, stockier of frame and younger, he had a glint of amusement in his eyes, a leer on his wet lips.

'Now thar's a skirt worth liftin'. Yessir, a little beauty an' already bedded to boot!'

'Not exactly, Coote. Greenbaum has played fair. But regrettably I've yet to impress the facts on her – that being agreeable is to her own good.'

Christine pushed up awkwardly off the bed's unevenly giving surface with a sob of disbelief. 'This is madness! You'll be made to pay–'

'No, young lady,' the major cut in sharply. 'I've already done my share of paying. Now you'll do your part by me. Business is business. Nasty things happen to people who welsh on their debts.'

'You can do nothing,' she said, lacking conviction, trying to bolster her courage. 'My mother taught me that a lady may take advantage of a gentleman, but a gentleman never, never presumes he can of a woman.'

Both men's response was scornful laughter.

'I don't know the story of your mother's life, but if that's a sample of her instruction, she was a damn fool,' said the major.

'Mama followed the teachings of her Saviour.'

'Come, come! We all know the sacredness of a young woman's chastity is purely an artificial convention. So an end to the shilly-shallying. You'll let me do as I please and like it. Unbutton your dress for a start!'

4

PAID OFF

'Let him take it howsoever he likes!'

Hustling the Rocking T cow critters along to their home range, Will Kearny acknowledged in his own mind that they were brave words. Bull Jusserand, like Arch Leggat said, was a mean piece of work. He'd made bloody wrecks of men who'd gone up against him. Some rumoured he'd also killed a woman – the girl Nita who'd disappeared mysteriously after the accidental death of her employer, the travelling medico Dr Holdstock.

The talk was she'd failed to please Franz Sturman and been passed over to Jusserand for punishment. She'd died and they'd gotten shed of her body secretly. It sounded kinda wild. Bunkhouse baloney. Sure, Sturman was tolerant of Jusserand's lapses and liked pretty women almost as much as other folks' land. But what of it?

Kearny couldn't blame Sturman for liking women. He enjoyed their company himself, though the chances for it were seldom.

The Rocking T ranch house sat on the side of a slope, down from a thick grove of cedars and chest-high sagebrush that were a windbreak when winter's storms charged through the valley from the rugged peaks away to the west.

Kearny had lately grown accustomed to a need to turn a blind eye to the run-down appearance of the house and outbuildings. That grated, but times were growing hard. When hands left, Thwaites told him not to replace them, which meant limits on anything but the most essential maintenance. The Rocking T was fighting for its existence and it showed in sun-blistered paint, corrals with broken poles and sagging fences.

All that Kearny saw now, but what registered first was the surrey in the uneven, rutted yard out front of the house. The two-horse team shuffled hoofs and switched tails at the flies. The horseflesh was of good stock; the four-wheeled carriage's paintwork a shiny black with gleaming brasswork and wheel spokes standing out in bright yellow.

Kearny turned in his saddle and said, 'I figure Pete's got visitors, Arch. I swear that fancy buggy belongs to Franz Sturman, no less.'

Leggat cursed. 'Sure don't belong around here. Ain't Rocking T's kinda rig. Sturman, huh? Yuh could be right at that.'

They drew closer. 'Yeah, it's Arrowhead all right,' said Kearny. 'I seen it around town.'

Leggat's puzzlement was plain. 'But Mr Stinkin' Sturman ain't the boss's kinda comp'ny. Ol' Pete ain't never bin one fer knucklin' under to the connivin', rattler-mean bastard! An' I figure Sturman's gonna be even less welcome when we tell how we caught Arrowhead scum red-handed run-nin' off Rocking T cows.'

'Well, it's our chance to let Sturman know the same as his boys – we've taken all we're going to take from them.'

It was a windy, a brag. Kearny knew it wouldn't be that easy to deal with Sturman. In truth, it wouldn't be easy at all.

Not two but three men looked round when Kearny showed up in the open door-way to Pete Thwaites's front parlour: the rancher himself, Franz Sturman and the Rawhide Fork attorney, Seabury Reece.

'Ah, Will ... come on in, will yuh?' Thwaites said.

Kearny sensed tension in the small room. The air was stale and oppressive. The smells of dust and neglect hung heavily in the confined space, contrasting with the scent drawn from the sage by the hot sun outside.

The occupants' eyes took in his battered appearance. It hadn't been much improved by a quick sluicing under the pump. The tension was spiked by curiosity.

Sturman arched his eyebrows and said, 'Why, howdy, Kearny. You don't look so good....'

Despite his words, the cattle baron's square, swarthy face held no sympathy.

'Don't fool at worrying 'bout me, Mr Sturman,' Kearny said coldly, bluntly. 'Your hired thug will need more patching up, and I figure you've got brass to come calling here.'

Sturman's face froze; not so much as an eyelid flickered. But Seabury Reece was a different kettle of fish. His sallow cheeks went a shade darker and his yellow-balled eyes, set close together, narrowed. His thin lips twisted.

'You speak in riddles, mister,' he said in a voice that creaked like an unoiled gate. 'If you're laying some kind of accusation against my client – my *friend* – I'd advise you in a legal capacity to have a care.'

'Aw, spare me the pretence, Reece. You and your employer know more than anybody about the dirty tricks the Arrowhead crew has been pulling on the Rocking T brand.'

Sturman glared at Kearny. 'I swear I don't know what you're talking about.'

'Then I'll tell you.' And that was what Kearny did.

While he talked, Sturman produced a cigar from a leather case, bit the end off and stuck it in the corner of his mouth. He made the best of listening in silence, giving his attention to firing up the cigar.

'Bullshit,' he said when Kearny had finished.

But Kearny figured he'd started sitting up and taking notice, especially when he got to Bull Jusserand's beating.

Reece, who wore a double-breasted, velvet-collared coat of black broadcloth despite the heat, tugged at its lapels and lifted his bony chin. 'Hmm! I'd want to hear the other side of this.'

But the least expected reaction was Pete Thwaites's. Kearny had thought the old man would be jubilant. Instead, he unclamped his stained teeth from the stem of his blackened corn-cob pipe and shook his head, his manner subdued.

'Waal, gents, I guess it don't make no

nevermind now,' he opined solemnly.

Kearny's searching eyes appraised him. He looked much as normal – his wrinkled face tanned to the colour and texture of an old saddle, his rope-scarred hands knobbly-knuckled yet still steady. But Thwaites's sharp eyes weren't meeting Kearny's and his shoulders were hunched under checked shirt and scratched rawhide vest. He gave the impression he was as washed out as the shirt and the red kerchief tied round his corded neck, both faded by sun and countless scrubbings.

Kearny didn't know how to take what he saw and heard. He said, 'No nevermind? I think Mr Sturman and his attorney should clear out of this house pronto!' His voice hardened with contempt. 'Their brains ought to tell them what my fists had to teach a thick-headed tough.'

The old rancher shook his head. 'Hold your hosses, Will. I jest agreed to sell out. I've had enough. All rights in the Rockin' T and its stock are passin' to Mr Sturman.'

Kearny's eyes sprang wide open, his jaw dropped. He couldn't hide his confusion.

Sturman and Reece exchanged smug glances.

'You've just...' Kearny began. 'What kind

56

of talk is this? Don't be a fool, Pete!'

'I'm not a fool. I'm quittin'. I'm gettin' shet of it afore it gets shet of me. It's the smartest thing to do.'

Thwaites swung across the room on his bowed legs and pulled a black metal cashbox from a bureau drawer. He dug out a thick roll of greenbacks. He slapped the paper money down on the scrubbed pine table in front of Kearny.

'That's everythin' I owe yuh, Will, an' pays yuh off. Leggat's is waitin' fer him in the box. Sam, Fu Yeng an' the rest of the crew have already gotten theirs an' lit out.'

Kearny's face clouded.

'You're crazy, Pete! The men will need their jobs. I need mine. You could use this kind of money to pay off some debt and keep the Rocking T afloat. I know I can make this spread work.'

Kearny shoved the bills back across the table.

Thwaites said, 'I'm not interested.' His tone was chilly as a spinster's rejecting a different kind of advance. 'Some thin's can't be did.'

Kearny felt like he'd absorbed another body blow from Bull Jusserand. His heart thumped. Old Pete tended to be a mite

57

eccentric, but Kearny thought he'd known his ways and had taken it without question that the salty rancher would stay rock-firm in holding onto his spread, no matter what Sturman might offer or throw at him.

Sturman flicked ash from his cigar. 'You got your walking papers, cowboy. Mr Thwaites is signing his deed over to me and I'm taking possession. I give you till daybreak to pull your freight.'

Reece smiled at Kearny greasily. 'Obviously, things panning out the way they have, there can be no job for you riding for Mr Sturman's Arrowhead brand.'

'If there was, you could stick it!' Kearny snapped. 'Pete, I know you ain't a man to walk away from things....'

Thwaites avoided his eye. 'Mebbe we should do it jest this once, Will,' he said, scowling. 'I guess you think I'm pretty gutless, not sittin' tight an' all.'

'You've done better than the most of them in this country, Pete,' Kearny allowed, puzzled as well as angry. 'But you can appreciate this puts me in a hole. The fact is, I'm a plain-dealing, working ranch foreman and it don't need saying there won't be a place for me around here anymore.'

Thwaites held out the roll of paper dollars

58

in a gnarled fist. 'You mind a word of advice? Take the goddamned money. Don't get to feelin' sorry for yuhself. An' don't stick around. It would be a lot smarter to quit this country whiles yuh fit and healthy.'

'The hell with advice! There's something very wrong with this. I just might hang around till I get to the bottom of it.'

Thwaites grew suddenly irritable. 'Now see here, let it drop! Yuh can't do any good. Sometimes a man has to let things go the way they's gotta go an' there ain't nothin' he can do 'bout it... Here, yuh'll need the money.'

Kearny felt sick that he could have misread the situation so badly.

He'd believed he'd understood Peter Thwaites and that he'd been his friend as well as his foreman. It had been a matter of pride in his job that he could judge men accurately.

Not interested...

He smelled deception in Old Pete's sudden turnabout, and as an honest, straightforward man he didn't like it. But maybe he was reacting immaturely, too sensitively; nobody liked rejection.

Kearny reluctantly accepted the money, nodding his thanks. From the corner of his eye he saw Sturman and Reece exchange knowing glances. The pair were up to something, for sure.

Reece cleared his throat. 'Lord, I hate to see a working man lose his livelihood, Mr Kearny.'

His grating whine did no more for Kearny than give the lie to his concern.

'Just maybe I could help out,' the lawyer went on. 'Something else could be in the offing. Call by my office in Rawhide Fork tomorrow morning. We could square this thing yet.'

'Stop beating the bushes, Reece.' Kearny strove to keep his voice expressionless. He had no stomach for letting Reece and his principal see how riled and vulnerable he felt. 'What's the deal?'

'Uh ... this isn't the moment, Mr Kearny. Like I say, tomorrow at my office would be time and place to outline the proposition.'

Kearny looked to Thwaites. The old man still wasn't meeting his glance, but he mumbled, 'Mebbe yuh should check it out, Will. Could be Mr Reece has it in mind to do yuh some favour.'

The devil he hasn't, Kearny thought.

Sturman shook his head gravely at Kearny's hesitation. 'You know, cowboy, the world is peopled by smart men and fools. There's a sucker missing his chances every minute. Sleep on that, and go see Mr Reece tomorrow.'

Kearny shrugged. 'Well, I guess you'll get me along, Reece. I've got no other choices hereabouts. I'm over a barrel.'

That and being plain inquisitive was the sum truth of it.

In his mouth was a taste more bitter than the blood and dirt swallowed in his clash with Bull Jusserand. Pete Thwaites had sold out to the enemy.

'I'd like it better if Kearny was dead,' Seabury Reece remarked. 'He smells like trouble.' He lifted his derby and mopped his brow with the linen square from his top pocket.

Franz Sturman's surrey was rolling back to Rawhide Fork, fried by a relentless noon-day sun and pursued by the rolling cloud of dust churned up by the jolting wheels. A hot, following wind occasionally propelled the dust ahead to swirl around the surrey's driver and passenger.

Sturman was unbothered by the heat and the dust. Or Kearny.

'We'll be shut of him fast enough now,

Reece,' he bragged. 'Settling his hash will fit perfectly into the grander scheme. Everything's shaking out just dandy. The mayor is toeing the line. The fund has been set up and newspaper advertisements we placed in the cities back East have drawn a heap of the kind of replies I anticipated right along.'

He grinned at the attorney, evil thoughts bringing a gleam to his eye.

Reece said, 'But Rawhide Fork has always been such a sleepy place. It seems hard to imagine how this will all work out...' His voice trailed away, ending his objection, if it was such, on a faint-hearted note.

Sturman's brash laugh dismissed his worries.

'You'll see, drybones. The Kearny fish is on your line and you just gotta play him along tomorrow. We'll turn the town into a Wild West hell-hole – and tie that smugly virtuous cowboy right into its ruin!'

5

DERRINGER VENGEANCE

'No! I'm too afraid. I'm not of that class...'

Faced by two strange and threatening men and with the demand to start undressing, Christine Smith prevaricated desperately in the grim New York tenement. She'd been a fool. Acting at being something she wasn't, she'd tacitly consented to surrender her virtue before she was allowed to return to her rented room at Eli Greenbaum's. She'd crossed the invisible line that divided the solid and outwardly respectable part of the city from the squalid and unseemly.

She sensed the initiative wouldn't be left to her more than moments.

She stood clutching the highest buttons of her simple purple dress.

Righteous, affronted, scared...

'Goddamn! I can't abide it, Major,' said Coote, sweat shining his face. 'Throwin' a shyness fit! Yuh paid fer her services an' she's gotta settle, no quibblin', no dickerin'.

Let's git on with learnin' her.'

'One last chance, my capricious maiden,' the major told Christine. 'Do you honour your part of our contract or do you renege?'

'How dare you speak of honour!' she flashed.

'That's it! Enough of this parley – I take my owings even if I have to hogtie you. Hold her, Sergeant!'

Coote closed on her, pulling her arms roughly behind her back. 'Yuh're sure beggin' to be took down a peg or two, gal.'

One thing Christine had learned in her relatively short life was that events took place which even as they unfolded you knew you'd want to forget but never would: the arduous wagon-train trek West as a child with her mother and father, the acrimonious scenes as her parents' relationship had fallen apart, the illness and death of her mother here back East.

Now there was this.

She struggled as best she could with her arms held fast behind her. But with surprisingly deft twists of his fingers, the major peeled the top of her dress and a daintily laced cambric chemise from her shoulders.

'Oh...! *Oh!*' Freed from restraint, her small, high-set breasts took on a bobbing life of their own. Shock and embarrassment stilled her tongue to a whimper; the men growled their pleasure.

'You filth!' she said, finding her voice.

'C'mon, gal,' Coote said. 'Yuh got it a-comin'. Let's see yuh perform fer sportin' gentry!'

He frog-marched her toward the bed, but she fought against him with all the strength she possessed. 'No! No!' she cried repeatedly, gripped by real terror. 'Let me alone!'

The sergeant could achieve no more than bending her forward over the framework of the bed-end. 'All right. We ain't pertik'ler how comf'table yuh'll be. Have it your way, wildcat!' In a bewildering change of tactics, he got on the bed and hauled her toward him by her aching arms.

Christine made a small, half-hysterical sound as her taut belly was dragged cruelly across the brass top rail until her hip bones bumped over it. She was upended; in-elegantly hinged at the pelvis, feet off the floor, bottom thrust high and her face plunged into the fusty-covered, goosefeather mattress. Any idea of retrieving modesty or dignity evaporated.

'Mercy!' she gasped in suffocating fear. 'This serves nothing!'

But the major grunted satisfaction and unbuckled his leather belt. 'On the contrary. There are a dozen different ways in which the thing might be done. Your choice affords us a magnificent spectacle and is as convenient as any.'

He tossed her skirt up over her back and grabbed her kicking right foot. He looped his belt around the ankle, then a vertical rod of the bedstead. 'Frisky mounts we tie,' he said. Pulling her legs apart and snatching his cravat off the chair, he secured her other ankle to a second rod, widely spaced from the first.

All the time, Coote kept pulling Christine's arms over her head. Once her ankles were tied, she felt that her limbs would be torn from their sockets.

Dread cracked her voice. 'Damn you! What are you doing?'

'You'll soon know, missy.' The major sounded jubilant and frighteningly confident. He pulled the loose ends of the drawstrings of her knickers, releasing the knot; then he hooked the fingers of both hands into the top of them and tugged the white cotton down her legs. 'Off – they – come!'

The drawers, though very full, were not made for forcible lowering down spread limbs. Seams gave with the heart-sinking ripping sound of sundered stitches and fabric. Christine screamed. 'God preserve me!'

But the choked prayer was unanswered.

Coote smacked his lips. 'Perfect ... Miss Snooty's got the makin's fer an extry fine strumpet.'

'Most tempting, Coote,' the major agreed. 'Let's show off her treasures royally!' He snatched up a pillow and Coote edged forward on his knees to permit enough slack in Christine's body for it to be pushed as a pad between the bed rail and her thighs.

Christine's skin crawled at their lewd guffaws and the thought of what was to come. Her futile fight was over. She was spread-eagled, brutally bent over the bed-end and completely available to whatever they wanted. Still sobbing inwardly, she made her body rigid and unresponsive, waiting for what was to be, detaching herself from her purgatory.

She heard the major snigger and step in behind. She didn't know what precisely to expect. He was taking her like an animal. But she was determined to be deflowered in absolute silence.

In the event, the feat proved impossible. She screamed out at the wounding and sank her teeth into the noisome bedcover.

After long, anguished moments, the major achieved his goal and his pleasure. In the big dresser mirror, she saw him backing away. 'Greenbaum delivered the goods,' he told his accessory wheezily.

The rape had destroyed her dignity and filled her with bitterness and pain, but now it was over with. She'd endured all life could bring. By repute, the fate was worse than death, though she didn't follow how anyone alive could know.

'I'm hurt,' she hissed. 'Let me loose, you – you dog!'

'Not yet, purty miss,' Coote said. 'Yuh've jest bin let up fer air. Take her arms, Major!'

'Oh, God, no!' Christine protested. With horror, she understood what the major had meant when he'd told her opposing him would make her trial twice as bad. In reward for his services, Coote was now to be given his way with her.

The major changed places with him on the bed, taking turn to grip her arms.

When Coote had been satisfied and the major let go of her arms, Christine saw that they were branded with purplish bruises from the men's vicious grips. She didn't dare think of other injuries.

'Untie my legs!' she blurted.

The major snickered as though, with his needs met, he was noticing her unladylike position for the first time. To complete her humiliation and squash any imagined vestige of pride, he dealt her several ringing slaps with the flat of his hand before moving round the bed to stoop and retrieve his belt and cravat.

'By God, that's how to show a balky filly the what-for of things!' he chortled. 'No prissy girl plays me for a sucker.'

Christine scarcely registered the stinging punishment or the ignominy. Her temper was white-hot. In fact, she'd suspended control over her feelings to the extent that balance had been tipped the other way. Her mind held no sway at all. She was in an insensate rage at the despicable thing they'd done to her.

The major was unfastening the belt; Coote, gloating and self-satisfied, was putting his legs back into his pants. 'Yuh gave her a grand lesson, Major,' he said. 'The look on her face was the funniest thing I ever did see!'

Patently they supposed that in her distress she would be harmless for a while, crushed by self-pity over the way she'd been used.

In their levity and contempt they misjudged hugely.

Wildness throbbed through her veins like it had been a powerful drug they'd injected into her body. The instant Christine's ankles were freed, she rolled forward. There was a whirl of limbs and lifted skirts, and she pounced from the bed.

Her objective was the one chair where the major's gun was draped in the soft leather of its shoulder rig with his coat.

Strained leg muscles cramped and gave way under her. The chair crashed over. She ended in a heap on the floor.

But still she grabbed the gun.

The smirks were wiped from the men's faces.

'Hey, put that thing down!' the major roared.

'Shit! The little baggage has gotten your pepper-pot, Major!' Coote, suspenders hanging loose, advanced on her recklessly.

Christine raised the strange, nickel-plated gun, holding it in both hands, pulling the hammer back with a thumb to cock it. It was a revolver of the derringer type and size favoured by gamblers. She'd not held a pistol in something like ten years; never fired one at a living target in her life. But the barrel came up in a steady arc, pointing at the broad chest coming toward her. She squeezed the trigger and the fat, stubby weapon bucked in her unpractised hands.

The firing of the gun reverberated deafeningly in the room. At close range the .44 slug punched a hole in Coote's tawdry green shirt, flinging him against the wall. Eyes and mouth agape, he slid down it, blood spurting from him.

The major must have seen that his victim was out of her head. He had the wit to make for the locked door, frantically groping in his pocket for the key.

Christine was completely cold to his fear and to Coote's ghastly death rattle. She calmly swung the derringer and it crashed again, spitting out its second load of doom.

The major rose to his toes, folded at the knees and fell headlong to the floor, where he rolled over. His face changed, losing its hectic blotches of colour. The lips peeled back from his teeth in a hideous travesty of the grins with which he'd ridiculed her. His bulging eyes accused her, but in seconds lost their focus, glazed by the nothingness of death.

The shots rang on in Christine's ears. An

acid taste was in her mouth. The full burden of her actions began to sink in.

She'd fatally shot two unarmed men, one in the back. But what did it matter? Given the beast-like manner of her ravishing, it was their just deserts. They'd forfeited life.

She realized she was still dumbly pointing the gun, as though she expected her despoilers to rise from their ugly deaths. She let her hands fall and dropped the gun as the blinding anger melted away, leaving a layer of cold perspiration on her brow.

A shiver shook Christine. She pulled up the top of her dress and straightened the skirt. She stood motionless, breathing deeply to still the sobs brought by her misery.

Nobody came. A shot or two … in this part of town, wise souls did not look into such occurrences. And thankfully she'd retained enough presence of mind not to take screaming flight down the stairs and into the street.

Though she felt no guilt, Christine experienced the first panicky awareness that she might be arrested for murder. Authorities might not take her part, especially if it came out that she'd had an assignation with the major; had in effect agreed to the sale of her virtue to him through Greenbaum. Not that she expected her landlord would lay information against her. He was way too smart to allow himself to be embroiled in anything as sordid or dangerous as vice and murders, even if bodies were found in a tenement he owned.

'I am not a murderess,' she told herself quietly.

But she was turned into a whore with rotten thoroughness. Stains on her ripped clothing testified that she was now a blooded member of that sisterhood, caught in the web of her own rashness. For though she'd changed her mind at the eleventh hour, she'd still become a fallen woman, her bills paid by the earnings.

Another concern entered her spinning head. No precautions had been taken. What if she found herself with child? Her shame would be revealed to the world.

She wanted to run. Not only from this squalid little room, but from her insecure home over Greenbaum's store and even from New York. She'd let herself be led onto a slippery slope. A future as a street girl had already loomed as a possibility; now she was condemned to be a fugitive, it seemed like destiny.

She'd seen a roundup once of the so-called flower girls. A troop of stern-faced Irish policemen had swept the streets at the behest of affronted city bigwigs. They'd crowded nigh on a hundred of the degraded and abused young women into a gloomy cell in the basement of their Broome Street station house.

No! Undone though she was, she couldn't endure that.

She sat down quietly on the sagging bed and avoided contemplation of her hollow-eyed reflection in the mirror. The clearest thought she could develop was that in every way it was unsafe to stay in New York. Previously she'd toyed with the idea that she must return to the West, look for the father her mother had walked out on and throw herself on his mercy. It now became a conviction that this was what she must do. Perhaps out West, away from the fraudulent pretensions and fripperies of the so-called polite society that had lured her departed mama, she would be able to enter on a new life with the past a closed book.

But the problem remained. Without means, the journey would be perilous. Could she even begin to make it?

6

ROBBED

Will Kearny had no cause to tarry. Arch Leggat had already made tracks and the deserted Rocking T bunkhouse had a spooky feel as he got his stuff ready to leave for the last time. Above his head, a rafter creaked like the popping of a distant rifle, shifting under the sun-baked shingles and tar paper. Dislodged by his gathering-up, some browned newspaper stuffed in a crack between warped siding boards fell to the dirt floor. There was no point in putting it back. This place was home to no one anymore.

After seven years of range life, Kearny's stuff didn't amount to much. It packed down into a couple of saddlebags and a bedroll. That and his saddle and the faded work clothes he wore. He guessed a cow-poke, even a top hand, didn't need more ... long as he had a job, some place with a bunk, a couple of shelves, a little wall space and a few hooks.

He stuffed the bills Thwaites had pressed on him into a wallet which he tied with a rawhide string. It went into a back pocket of his pants, making a bulge. The roll would last a while, which was a reassurance. Kearny was not the kind who could stomach being beholden to others or a recipient of charity. In particular, he wanted his options open when he faced Seabury Reece. He was intrigued to know what the attorney had to offer, but unless it was to his liking, it would give him pleasure to turn the man down.

If anyone in Rawhide Fork and its environs had legal business to do, Reece was their only choice. But the one-horse town was scarcely litigation-minded and Reece was deeply into estate and land deals.

Kearny suspected his practice thrived through sharp practice; he made it pay by fleecing folks who were not in a position to do much about it. He did them down without scruple, masking his dishonesty with a smarmy charm.

The one man who'd gotten the lawyer's measure was Franz Sturman. Reece served the powerful rancher with sycophantic zeal. Could be he feared Sturman. Or Sturman represented the best pickings since he was the wealthiest person around.

No ceremony attended Kearny's departure. Old Pete watched him mount his mustang. 'Why don't yuh take the black?' Thwaites said, offering an olive branch. 'He's a younker come out of a part-Kentucky strain an' yuh're welcome.'

Kearny shrugged. He excused his refusal with a prejudice common among cow-business wranglers. Black horses looked good on the outside but too many failed to live up to the promise in performance. You did best picking only those who'd proven themselves through and through. 'I know the chestnut because he's my own,' he said. 'He's the best cutting horse I ever had. Got a sight of bottom, too, and I can always tell what he's going to do just by watching his ears. But thanks all the same.'

The sun was westering, the shank of the afternoon spent when Kearny headed out for the town where he would stop at least one night. He touched his favourite chestnut with blunted spurs, easing the horse into a lope.

Horse and man's shadow lengthened as he rode the dusty yellow trail to town. The thing that gripped him most was the sudden, uncharacteristic way his boss had closed his books and quit. He'd had faith in Thwaites. But Old Pete must be nudging seventy and fed up with strife. Could a younger man in conscience blame him? Sturman and the hard bunch he'd signed on were a mean crowd to fight.

Yet Kearny couldn't make up his mind that this was the sum of it.

And despite the thick roll of dollar bills stretching the denim against the copper rivets in his pants, he also studied on whether he'd been paid his entire dues. He'd been on Thwaites's place seven years. He'd done his share of rounding-up, branding, castrating calves, dehorning, hauling stuck cows from boggy waterholes. Gotten frozen in winter and scorched in summer looking after Old Pete's interests. And all the time he'd had to put up with the rancher himself. He wasn't exactly a loveable codger with his scratchiness and stubbornness.

Sturman's takeover of the Rocking T must gall Pete, surely. 'Guess it ain't rightly no concern of mine you'll be sickened when it sinks in what you've done,' Kearny told an absent audience. 'I offered to pitch in with what I had to whip 'em, but you said you wasn't interested, and that's as far as it can go.'

Maybe the fact was he should have walked out on Old Pete years back, staked out a claim in his own behalf, taken himself a wife. He laughed aloud at his ponderings. A wife! He'd nothing to give a woman if one was offering.

Lost in his musings, Kearny rode the chestnut at a rocking-chair lope, the experienced range man's customary gait. He made nothing of it when he caught a glimpse way ahead of a lone rider skylined on a knoll from where a man might survey the trail that snaked across the rangeland to Rawhide Fork. When he looked again, the rider had gone, leaving only a faint hint of hoof-churned dust. Moments later grouse left the timber on the knoll's far slopes, beating up on hard rapid wings.

By the time he reached town, Kearny's anger at his dismissal by Thwaites was evaporating into the sage-scented air of coming dusk. He was left with just an irritating sense of failure.

Rawhide Fork had but one saloon, the barn-sized First Claim. Kearny noticed that some of the dozing saddle horses at the hitching-rail outside the drab premises carried Arrowhead brands, but he didn't give it much thought since it was something to be ordinarily expected. One animal gave off more warmth than the others, like it was a recent arrival. Drying lather showed at the edges of the saddle blanket.

He swung down and looped the chestnut's reins around the rail. Even the stiffness that lingered from the bruising clash with Bull Jusserand failed to warn him that he could be walking into trouble when he pushed through the batwings.

He was intent on flushing the dryness from his throat and catching up on the gossip of the territory. Anything that promised the chance of a job would be of prime interest.

Two hanging lamps cast a feeble light over the smoky interior. The fumes of spilled liquor and the stink left by sweaty bodies seemed to seep out of the shabby furnishings and the sawdusted floor to augment the tobacco fug.

There was also an air of expectancy; a brittle quiet of watching and waiting.

Kearny adjusted his eyes to the gloom and saw the bunch of Arrowhead hardcases clustered around Bull Jusserand at the bar. It was too late to turn back, even had he been so minded.

'Now don't do nothing hotheaded, boys,' said one of the two shirtsleeved men behind the bar. This was Seth Mallison, owner of the First Claim, a sallow-complexioned man carrying no surplus flesh, a perpetually mournful expression like he had secret griefs, bushy hair parted in the middle and a moustache that was thick and drooping. The other man, a rotund barkeeper, was trying to hide behind his boss's spare frame.

Jusserand ignored Mallison and glared at Kearny. Despite the licking he'd taken that day, the man mountain's bloodshot eyes were no less crafty and vindictive than usual. The ugly hulk had enviable powers of recuperation. He thumped the bottle he held down on the bar and cleared himself a space among his pals, spreading his big feet wide. He wiped the back of a hairy hand across his mouth and said, 'Waal, lookee here, it's the smart bastard hisself! I hear yuh got orders to drift, *Mister* Kearny. How come yuh git to drag your ass inta *workin' men's* comp'ny?'

Kearny cursed under his breath. He could do without this aggravation.

'No one's running me out of any town, Jusserand. You mind your own business and keep your sticky beak out of mine.'

Baldy Hogsden, who was leaning indolently against the bar behind Jusserand, stopped a rhythmic chewing and opened his brown-stained mouth. 'Yuh hear that, Bull? He called your nose a sticky beak. He got lucky this mornin'. Now he reckons he can give yuh any crap!'

Jusserand's thick lips twisted into an evil grin. 'Why, yeah ... that's an *insult*, Kearny, an' this time I'm gonna beat yuh into a splatter!'

The thug shambled forward some more, his big shoulders hunched, his long arms hanging slack. Kearny realized then he'd let himself be set up the way the Arrowhead bunch had fixed. It was plain as hoofprints in mud but too late to be remedied. He was in for one hell of a fight.

Kearny knew better than to back off. He moved in swiftly, feinted with his right and followed with a smashing left.

Jusserand was caught off guard with his ham-sized paws still dangling at his sides. But he shook off the punch and the mirthless grin stayed on his blotched face. He licked his lips in anticipation as Kearny raised his fists in front of his face to fend off the retaliatory blow. Then with a speed surprising for a man of his bulk, Jusserand shot out his long arms and wrapped them round Kearny in a rib-cracking clinch.

Kearny rained blows at Jusserand's head, but the range was too short to get any force behind them, and Jusserand only increased the pressure. Desperately, losing his breath fast, Kearny jerked up his knee.

Jusserand laughed as the knee contacted his mid-section, doing no more damage than Kearny's flailing fists. His laugh turned to a roar when Kearny brought the reinforced high heel of his riding boot down on his instep – hard.

Kearny felt the grip that held him slacken. And that was all he needed. He used both his arms to lever himself off Jusserand's chest. Jusserand, tottering on his pained foot, swiped Kearny's left temple with a wildly thrown fist as the ex-Rocking T man broke the hold and staggered backwards, free.

The thump to Kearny's head started bells ringing and lights flashing.

It also sent him reeling into the Arrowhead rannies. In the jostle, they digged him and jabbed his kidneys with sly punches before flinging him back at their bully boy.

'Knock 'im cold, Bull,' said Baldy Hogsden. 'Then we'll open his pants, castrate him an' stuff his balls in his big mouth!'

Kearny went straight into a legs-buckling

jaw-cruncher from Jusserand. The room tilted and the floor rushed up to hit him in the backside.

'I saw that, Baldy! It was dirty. Yuh pushed Will Kearny.'

A familiar voice cut through the ringing in Kearny's ears. He rolled onto his knees. He shook his head to clear his eyes of the swimming blackness.

Unnoticed, Arch Leggat had stepped through the batwings. He stood just inside the saloon, his knotty fist weighted with Colt iron, his leathery face grim and set.

'Stand right where yuh are, the lot o' yuh, an' thet means *you*, too, Bull Jusserand! This here ain't no fair fight an' it's broken up... Any sonofabitch thinkin' diff'rent gits a slug in the brisket, y' unnerstand?'

Incredibly, one Arrowhead man in the deeper shadows went for his gun, taking a chance his recklessness would go unnoticed by Leggat until it was too late. Kearny saw him first. Coming to his feet and still groggy, he surprised even himself with the quickness of his response.

His greased draw baffled the eyes of Leggat and the gang he covered. The Arrowhead gun drawer could have seen only a blur as Kearny's long-barrelled .45 left its open-topped holster. The crash of gunfire split the thick air twice in rapid succession.

The second crash, drowning the thundering echo of the first, came from the Arrowhead weapon. It exploded with a flash of flame as it flew from the ranny's suddenly nerveless hand. His wrist was drilled and broken. He howled.

'You asked for it, mister,' Kearny said. 'Mebbe your pals will help you along to Doc Oram's. 'Cause now Leggat and me are saying whose company's acceptable in here – and we're saying yours ain't! The whole damn rat-pack of you can do your drinking in some other hole.'

But Kearny wasn't having the last word, even though he had the drop on the Arrowhead crowd. Unexpectedly, Seth Mallison's hands dived under his counter to reappear clutching a shotgun.

'Now just you hold it, Will Kearny,' Mallison said. 'This here's a mean piece of armament and I'm a nervous man with a business to run. Any marching orders come from me.'

Kearny frowned. 'Well, this is a surprise, Mr Mallison. Forgive me for acting out of turn, but I was thinking you didn't have the guts to keep these premises peaceable.'

The pudgy barkeep bobbing about behind Mallison gulped and swabbed his sweaty, hairless head with the cloth he used to mop slops off the bar.

Mallison looked morbid as an undertaker behind the unwavering, twin twenty-eight-inch barrels of the Remington shotgun. 'I don't know about that, Kearny, but this ten-gauge says I'm the one calling the shots from here on. Both barrels are loaded. Both cocked. Fast as you swung that forty-five on me, I'd still cut you in half. And I says it's you and your sidekick Leggat who pull their freight. You're washed up here anyways.'

Kearny stiffened. 'You've joined Sturman's clique, huh? You're one of them now, is that it?'

Mallison's weary eyes fixed Kearny's, haunted by all the ghosts of his yesterdays. A born loser.

'I'm just a prudent man, Kearny,' he said. 'I believe in surviving. Think about it. I'm saving your skin, too. You're through. If you set any store by your health, you'll ride out of this country before they start beating the bushes for you.'

Kearny nodded. 'I get the picture. Business is business. Money talks. I guess you don't appreciate that somewhere, some-

86

time, a man with sand has to make a stand.'

'I ain't the fighting kind, Kearny.'

'No ... and I predict you'll live to regret licking these bullies' dirty boots, but by then it'll be too late to get out from under.' Kearny was fuming, but he kept a rein on his rising temper. 'We'll let it lie, Arch. The smell around here would spoil having a drink anyhow.'

Kearny edged round to join Leggat and the pair backed out.

'Sure goes agi'nst the grain backin' down to scum,' Leggat muttered on the plankwalk outside. Jeers and hollers issued from the Arrowhead men left in possession. The brittle light of anger made Leggat's eyes like bits of broken glass in his weather-beaten face.

'I'm mad myself but Mallison's way makes a certain amount of sense,' Kearny admitted. 'They'd got the numbers and would've had us bailed up in there once we'd booted 'em out.'

Whereupon Leggat let loose a stream of profanity about the injustice of their lot, and Kearney diplomatically reminded him that he'd saved his, Kearny's, bacon – 'I sure owe you, Arch' – and suggested they took a room for the night at Rawhide Fork's Stardust

Hotel and let the situation cool off.

But they got no closer to a hotel room than the lobby. 'Evenin', gentlemen,' said the clerk. 'A room? That'll be two dollars the night in advance.'

Kearny reached for the wallet in his pants pocket, tightly packed with his payoff from Pete Thwaites. And his face went the colour of cold ashes.

The money was gone! Now his tail was really in a crack.

'The thievin' bastards!' Leggat yelled, riled up anew. 'Let's git back to that saloon. We want your *dinero,* an' if Mallison don't like it, he kin stick it up his ass!'

Without ado, they rushed out into the street and back to the First Claim Saloon. But they were too late. It was full dark, the Arrowhead horses were gone from the hitchingrail, and the plump barkeep felt brave enough to gloat over telling them that Bull Jusserand and his pards had larruped out of town with whooping yells just moments before.

7

'THIS TOWN NEEDS WOMEN!'

'Sit down, Kearny.' Seabury Reece waved Will Kearny into a chair facing his desk. A gold signet ring on his little finger caught the early morning sun streaming through his office window. His linen collar gleamed a spotless white.

Kearny was aware of the shabbiness of his range garb; the scabbed splits and colourful contusions on his face from the fights with Louey Jusserand of the day before. Setting himself down, he reflected silently that these things mattered not a hoot. His want of Reece's sleek niceties would not allow the lawyer to intimidate him. What he did rue was the loss of his thick roll of dollars and the independence it had represented.

'Let me hear what you had on your mind, Reece,' he said brusquely.

'A cigar, Kearny?' Reece asked, ignoring his visitor's uncouth bid to get down to cases without polite preliminaries. He pushed a fancy cedarwood box across his polished mahogany desktop.

Kearny shook his head and dug a sack of Bull Durham from his shirt pocket. He produced a wheatstraw paper and shaped up a cigarette from these makings with studied care, leaving Reece to contemplate his failure to open with small talk.

Reece drew back aloofly in his chair, which had a high, carved back and was upholstered with overstuffed calfskin.

The silence had ridden on some and Kearny was thumbnailing a lucifer before Reece overcame his obvious irritability. 'I see your face is even more – ah – battered than I saw it yesterday,' he ventured. 'More fighting with Mr Sturman's men, I understand.'

'What do you know about that?' Kearny asked, his eyes slitting. He sucked in a lungful of harsh smoke and flicked the charred matchstick toward a fireplace.

'Why, the whole town is abuzz about the ruckus, Kearny.'

'You wouldn't also happen to know what became of my payroll from Thwaites, would you? Was it pickpocketed on your Mr Sturman's orders?'

Reece bristled. 'Are you making an allegation, Kearny? I'll warn you, as I did just yesterday, to watch your speech lest your unfounded figurings mire Mr Sturman's reputation.'

'And what if I don't give a damn for Sturman's good name – if he has one?'

'Mr Sturman is a big man through the breadth of this basin.'

Kearny's smile was sardonic. 'Wider in his own estimation.'

'Mr Sturman has power in the Cattle Raisers' Association,' Reece said, ignoring Kearny's brazen insult. 'If he gets you blacklisted, you can't expect to work again in the territory's cow business – ever. No, sir, it won't do to throw your dirt at Mr Sturman. Slander is a serious crime.'

'Thieving likewise,' Kearny said, but moderating his belligerence to firmness. 'I was minded to lay a complaint with Marshal Gurney is all, 'cept he seemed absent from his office. Where has he gotten to? He should've been laying down the law last night to those Arrowhead yahoos.'

A thin smile creased the lawyer's sallow face. 'You can forget Amos Gurney, Kearny. He has vacated his office in every sense. Rawhide Fork has no use for a town marshal.'

'Yeah?' said Kearny, incredulous. 'Who says?'

'It was a decision of last week's meeting of the town council on the casting vote of Mayor Martinez,' Reece stated smugly. 'These small-town peace officers are a sorry breed mostly, out for what they can get.'

'Gurney was an honest lawman in my book,' Kearny said.

'Be that as it may, the mayor and council are taking a fresh line on law and order. Rawhide Fork being *generally* peaceable' – Reece paused for another distasteful appraisal of Kearny's fight-battered visage – 'the town has chosen not to renew the marshal's contract.'

Kearny's expression was bleak with scorn. 'Huh! More likely, the so-called good citizens of Seth Mallison's stripe couldn't abide putting up the money that paid his wages.'

Reece might have a furtive, uneasy way with him, but today he seemed to collect more confidence from everything Kearny said. 'Wrong, Kearny! They're of a persuasion to end the drain on their pocketbook and put their hard-earned dollars where they won't be wasted – behind a better idea.'

'What's that?'

'A grand scheme to boost this no-account burg from a small, dead place to an expanding community with thriving prospects.'

Kearny took a deep drag on his hand-rolled quirly, let the smoke dribble from between half-parted lips. 'You got a hell of a roundabout way of answering questions, lawyer man. Why don't you just spit out what's in mind without the fancy talk? Who put up this scheme?'

Reece coughed as though modesty constrained him. 'The authors were largely Mr Sturman and myself, but it was recognized and wholeheartedly adopted by a body of men whom I might describe at the very least as your peers, if not betters.'

Kearny let the slight go by. 'And how exactly does it do what you say?'

He was considering how Rawhide Fork would look to a seasoned outsider: just one more cow town, a sprawl of weather-warped frames and old 'dobes, of falsefronts and plankwalks, a roadway with three inches of dust or mud puddles, depending on the season. Better-placed cattle towns, like Dodge City, Abilene and Ellsworth, would have a quarter, often on the brow of higher ground, from where a select minority of the richer and more respectable citizens could look down, hitching up their skirts from the vulgar source of their prosperity. Rawhide Fork had nothing like it. At best, it was a hard-working, unlovely place.

Built from scratch by cattlemen, it had no history, unlike its nearest neighbour town, Jamesville, a half-day's ride away. There, the new town had been built around the nucleus of a fort-like adobe village, generations old, which was now its 'Mex-town' quarter.

Reece might have been reading his mind. 'The premise is simple to men of vision and foresight, Kearny. Rawhide Fork lacks stability and gentility, and the key to these things is the Fairer Sex.' He pronounced the words with audible capitals.

Kearny's jaw must have dropped. 'Uh?'

'To hit straight to the point of things, this town needs more women! Many more of them.'

Kearny stroked his stubbly chin. It was true womenfolk were in short supply. That was the same all over the West. The lures of the cattle industry and the gold and silver rushes had been to men. Only one out of every three immigrants was a woman.

Many women couldn't endure the primitive conditions, the scarcity of manufactured comforts and the long periods of loneliness. It was worst for those who had to help their men wrest a living from the raw land. The outdoor chores were a never-ending round.

The wife of a small rancher or homesteader was expected to tend the essential garden patch, care for the domestic livestock, bear his children. The beauty of youth quickly faded. Fair skin was weathered by the sun and the desert winds, the heat and the cold, so that the look of old age came long before time. Some went back East. Others died of illness or in childbirth, or of the sheer godawful drudgery in a harsh climate. Most survivors were dried-up, wrinkled crones.

New Mexico Territory had the Mexicans' womenfolk, of course. While young, they were some of the world's most stunningly beautiful females by the ideals of any race. Vivacious and fun-loving, with sparkling dark eyes and flashing smiles, most were expressive charmers who made love with natural grace and hot-blooded passion. Formal marriages with *Mestizos* or fully Spanish-blooded Mexicans did occur, but for many Anglos racial intermingling was a hypocritical affair. You might sleep with a *perdida* in a border brothel but marry a *señorita*, let her give you brats – hell, no.

Reece whipped a report paper from a desk drawer and flourished it.

'In 1870, Arizona had one woman to every four men over age twenty-one; Wyoming, one to every six; Idaho and Montana one to every eight... I could go on throughout the entire West, Kearny. But what's plain to this town is that it must rectify the imbalance in order that its men are able to marry, set up homes and start families – in short, bring civilized and regulated living to its environs. Until then we will have the rootlessness and shabbiness, also the petty crimes and fights of bored cow-hands.'

'Them's fine sentiments, Reece, but Rawhide Fork ain't set up for ladies with their needs and vanities. Why, the town don't even have no millinery, dressmaking or suchlike emporium. Ain't logic to expect women to come looking here.'

Reece smiled softly. 'We ain't – *are not* – waiting for them to. The town is financing the insertion of notices in prominent newspapers back East, like the *Herald* and the *World* in New York. Our message is addressed to widows, orphans and the unemployed.'

'In a big city that covers a lot of folks,' Kearny said.

'We stipulate that for free, escorted passage to a life of promise they need to be unmarried females between ages seventeen and twenty-five.'

Kearny frowned and shook his head from

side to side wonderingly. 'What has this deal to do with me?'

'The first – um – cargo of brides will arrive shortly at the Lamy railroad depot out of Santa Fe. A reliable, resourceful representative, namely yourself, must ride there to meet the party and bring it safely down-country to Rawhide Fork. A stagecoach will be privately chartered for the journey back. Expense money will be provided in advance.'

Kearny laughed disbelievingly. 'Hell, I herd cows – not women! I ride a horse, throw a loop, slap on a branding-iron. Those skills I savvy.'

'But as of yesterday there's no range work for you in these parts, Kearny. If I were you, I'd think seriously before you refuse. The town is putting up two hundred dollars for the job. Nigh on a common cow-hand's wages for six months.'

A silence took hold. Kearny was tempted, but the feeling that he'd not gotten a full explanation of Reece's motives brought a dryness to his throat. Nervousness? Premonition?

Last night, shunning a loan from Arch Leggat, he'd unrolled his blankets and bedded down in the livery barn loft, courtesy of an obliging hostler. He didn't know how long he could rely on that frugal hospitality.

At last he said with a lift of his shoulders, 'All right. I'm hired. It doesn't figure right to me. Preposterous, sort of. But I guess since I got ambushed in the First Claim, I don't have the coin to be a no-sayer.'

'That's smart thinking, Kearny. It's not often the man whose circumstances have been so completely wiped out can expect to have such a chance dropped in his lap.'

Kearny leaned forward and crushed out the end of his smoke in a cut-glass ashtray. 'Talk on, Reece. I want all the details of this plumb straight, so there's no mistakes.'

'Sure, Kearny, I do admire a thorough approach.'

Reece clasped his hands together, settled his elbows on his desk and droned on for a while, filling in the gaps.

By the time Kearny left the stuffy office, he had an itinerary, a sixty-dollar advance and a fuller picture of the novel plan. Also a day in hand, it seemed. And that would allow him to do some quiet checking out. For though acting as a chaperon didn't sound even mildly dangerous, he had a suspicion his neck had been shoved into a noose. The trickiest part would be ducking out fast if someone tried to yank up the slack.

8

CHRISTINE'S CHANCE

Christine ignored the alarming fact that the dilapidated mansion had every appearance of what her mother would have called a house of ill-fame. The promise of the advertisement in the newspaper had been too good to be true, coinciding so exactly with her desire to be transported West at no charge. And of all places – to Rawhide Fork itself. She'd no wish to spoil such a glowing prospect of salvation with the trepidation that nibbled at the fringes of her mind.

The street, on New York's Lower East Side, was mean and ugly, but the decor inside the mansion was ornate except that it was tawdry with age and needed some maintenance. Christine's first impression was of overstuffed silk cushions, furniture with curved legs, red velvet draperies and cloying perfume. An atmosphere of decadence.

The woman who interviewed her introduced herself as Miss Temperance Doe. She was brash and buxom and had bottle-bleached hair like brittle straw. She made no bones about the place being a bordello.

Christine put on a bold face. 'As long as the trip to New Mexico is truly forthcoming, I can endure anything meantime,' she said.

'New Mexico is a long way to ship goods,' Miss Doe said. 'Rawhide Fork needs the best prospects, like childless young widows or deserted wives with plenty of wear left in 'em an' itching to trade. Women with their pride sapped by the relentless devil of abstinence. Needful women.'

'I am in dire need, ma'am. I've spent too many days' fruitless searching for jobs, sleeping between backstreet trash barrels and living on the scraps of rotten food I've found in them.'

Miss Doe looked at her dubiously. 'I can't use innocents.'

'My innocence has been lost, I assure you, ma'am. I've done no grieving for it.'

What she didn't say was that such grieving was a luxury for which she'd been allowed no chance. What, anyway, would have been the use? She told Miss Doe half-truths, insinuating she knew much more about the trade in sexual pleasure than she'd acquired from her defloration and the talk of the girls she'd been forced to mix with on the streets since.

And, of course, she said nothing that would reveal she was a fugitive murderer. It was still her constant prayer that if there was a merciful God, He would understand and forgive her terrible sin. Like every victim – and especially as a victim who'd exacted retribution – she was troubled by guilt for what had happened to her.

'Well, I'm telling you straight – backlands folk can't hand out tickets to finicky girls who have to be taught how to behave,' said Miss Doe. 'Pushy cowmen are in too big a hurry for fancy courting. The knight of the frontier who sets womankind on a pedestal an' worships their purity is just sugar-coated, dime-novel bunkum put about by hypocrites. It will be no overtures an' into the action lickety-split where we're going.'

After Christine had accepted Miss Doe's offer and its conditions, shaking inside but excited, too, she was taken to a steamy bathhouse, a frame building attached to the rear of the mansion.

Miss Doe had delegated two girls to see that she was made clean and 'free of vermin'. Christine recognized from their type that the girls were practised prostitutes. They were both older than herself with figures more developed than her own slight frame.

Her shyness about stripping off in front of them was ameliorated by the luxurious thought that at last she was going to wash off the grime of city low-life.

Moonshine shafted down the alley behind the First Claim Saloon. The cold silver light cast stark shadows between heaps of empty crates and trash, but was adequate to show Kearny the rear door, etching the flakes of drab, peeling paint and revealing a worn latch. A cautious jiggle told him the latch wasn't off the hook.

The saloon had closed for business but a lamp still burned in Seth Mallison's living quarters out back. Kearny debated whether he should knock up the saloon man but decided against it. Best no one else should know about the enquiries he planned to make.

Patience, a little savvy and a thin-bladed knife opened the door for him. He entered a storeroom, dark as the inside of a boot and smelling like one that had been worn for a long, hot day. He paused to let his eyes adjust, satisfied only when he could make out objects around him.

Kearny was an outdoors man. He felt keenly the claustrophobia of the close walls and ceiling, and that he'd entered as an intruder.

He negotiated the hulking obstruction of a stack of unopened paint pails and eased open the door to the lighted room beyond.

Mallison was slouched over the table in his back room. From between his slack lips jutted a dead stogie; on the much ring-marked pine in front of him stood a near-empty quart bottle of Old Crow bourbon flanked by a used glass.

'Howdy, Mallison,' Kearny said quietly, civilly.

Mallison near swallowed his stogie. He spat it out, jerking to his feet. His eyes, wild as a spooked jackrabbit's, settled on the knife Kearny had neglected to return to the sheath in the top of his boot.

'What the blazes do you want, Kearny?'

'I want some answers.'

Mallison didn't understand, linking the nocturnal visit to the bar-room confront-ation of the day before. 'You carve me up, folks'll know it was you!'

'I ain't here to settle no scores. You're a member of the town council and I've got questions to ask.'

'You're busted down to an unruly saddle bum, mister. Council business ain't none of your'n,' Mallison growled, starting to get a grip on his trembling.

'This is, seeing's how lawyer Reece has hired me on to fetch a party of council-sponsored immigrant women to town.'

Some of the fear in Mallison's eyes was replaced by sullen wariness.

'What do you know about that?'

Kearny told him. 'But that's not enough. Why are you ginks putting the town's money and name behind Sturman's scheme?'

'It don't seem such a bad idea is part of it,' Mallison said. 'Rest is, Sturman's got influence. Reece is just a fee-lawyer in Sturman's pocket, but he drew up smart mortgages over my saloon and a raft of other Rawhide Fork enterprises, including Mayor Martinez' mercantile. It happened during the four-year drought when most of the basin's cowmen were near broke and business was bad. The loaned money that pulled us through came from Sturman.'

Kearny nodded. 'So you haven't got the guts to turn him down.'

'We ain't taking chances. Sturman's the meanest and greediest galoot on God's earth. He'd foreclose. Crazy feuding with him ruined all this range's small operators. It won't happen to us.'

'Pete Thwaites had the grit to buck him,' Kearny said.

Mallison sneered. 'Bankrupted hisself doing it. You know most about that. Look at him now. Sold out like the rest, like as not on worse terms.'

Kearny decided Mallison was telling it like it was and that he could learn nothing more here. The saloon keeper had confirmed what Reece had told him, but added little. He slipped his knife back into its sheaf.

'You don't take sides, do you?' he said. 'You just deal with whoever looks like the winner.'

Mallison was unaffected by Kearny's disgust. His sallow face wore the cocky grimace that was the nearest he ever came to a grin as Kearny backed out of the room the way he'd come.

Kearny's mind whirled in the thick gloom. So few answers. So many more questions.

Old Pete Thwaites's whole life had been built around the Rocking T. It was meat and drink to him. Why had he thrown in the towel to a range hog? It didn't make a lick of sense.

Franz Sturman was a landed cattle baron – successful, prosperous, a power in the territory. Driven by personal ambition, his reputation hadn't been built on playing the public benefactor. This was what puzzled Kearny most. Sturman wasn't the type to take an interest in improving others' lives or developing the fabric of Rawhide Fork society. His breed didn't know the meaning of philanthropy. What was his game?

Kearny just couldn't figure it. His livelihood lost, all he could do was play along, and maybe he would find answers.

9

MISCHIEF IN SANTA FE

An hour after he'd ridden his leg-weary chestnut into Santa Fe and hunted up a livery where he could leave it, Will Kearny was lying back in a barbershop chair, his two-day stubble freshly lathered. He'd already taken a hot soak in a hotel bath and was therefore well into the 'duding up' process familiar from his trail-herding days. Soon he'd be fit to rub shoulders with townsfolk.

A wizened little barber stropped the razor and tested its sharpness on his thumb. Kearny noted with approval that although the man was advanced in years, his hand was still rock-steady.

'Kearny, eh?' the barber said. 'Any relation to the late famous General Stephen Watts Kearny?'

'Not that I know of.'

'It was Kearny took Santa Fe offa the Messicans way back in '46. Built that thar

Fort Macy, up the hill behind the governor's palace. Smart man was General Kearny. Nary a drop o' blood spilled. Didn't mess none with the Spanish-Indian traditions. They was left their own habits and religion, y' foller.'

Kearny grunted assent as the ancient barber swished the razor through the suds on his jaw. For himself, he'd found Santa Fe much as he'd always known it during his shorter adulthood. Though under the American flag for decades, the native Hispanos continued to outnumber the Anglos.

The barber turned to rinse the razor. 'The railroad must've brought some changes though,' Kearny probed.

'Aw... not so notably as in other places, friend. They might've called it the Santa Fe Railroad – pre'xactly the Atchison, Topeka and Santa Fe – but the town has proven a kinda backwater in the railroad age. The route westward is unsuitable, yuh see. What we got is a branch line, the main one bein' put through Albuquerque.'

Kearny knew that Kansas City, at the other end of the Santa Fe Trail, had been reached by the iron rails in 1875, but it had taken another five years before the Santa Feans had seen their first train. He also knew of the bitter clashes between the Santa Fe and the D & RG – short for Denver and Rio Grande Western Railroad – for supremacy in the railroad business in the South-West. Legal battles, fist fights and shootings took place over rights to run tracks through rocky mountain passes.

His barber informant could reel the nation's facts and figures off his busy tongue.

'Did yuh know? When the War 'tween the States ended in 1865, there was only thirty-five thousand miles of track. A sight less'n a dozen years after, double that many was in use.'

Kearny nodded. 'They do say the trains are building America. They've changed this territory for certain sure.'

'Yeah, the old Spanish aristocrats used to raise sheep mostly. With the coming of the railroads, we got ourselves a cattle boom, I guess.'

Running on at the mouth, he allowed that while this had changed the practices of landed families, the *rancheros* and their *vaqueros* clung to an age-old feudal set-up yet. But the boom had also brought in the *Norte Americano* cowboys, like Will Kearny, and created a few cattle barons, like John

Chisum on the Pecos River.

And Franz Sturman in Rawhide Fork's environs, Kearny silently appended. Well curried, his outlook improved, Kearny left the barbershop and struck back through the crooked streets of the territorial capital toward the railroad depot. Santa Fe, with its centuries of history and the presence of Roman Catholicism, was not as wide open as raw trail towns Kearny had known, but the place was buzzing round the clock, it seemed. People crowded the sidewalks about the plaza, and the gambling houses, saloons and dance halls which had sprung up to cater to the immigrants were doing lively business.

Kearny wasn't inclined to spend or chance any of the coin he carried. He didn't rightly know how long it was going to have to last him, or what other demands might be put on it. In plenty of time, he headed directly for the rendezvous Seabury Reece had set up at Lamy with the incoming train bringing passengers from Kansas City and points east.

In 1866, 5000 freight wagons had travelled across the Great Plains to Santa Fe. Now, the freighters' mode of transport was made obsolete; soon, with iron tracks spreading across the map like the web of a drunken spider, even stagecoach lines hereabouts would follow them into oblivion.

Kearny was not the only man waiting at the station. A mixed bunch of businessmen had already gathered on the platform. Some had the hooded eyes and high cheekbones of Indians; others had Mexican looks; one was a fair-skinned Nordic.

They spoke between themselves in a mixture of tongues. Kearny didn't savvy all he heard, but what came out of the intelligible jargon was that these men, too, were all waiting for young girls arriving by the train.

Their coarse talk made Kearny uneasy.

Every one of them was a bad lot, he estimated. They were dance-hall owners, bordello landlords or pimps. What they all had in common, regardless of race or language, was that they were nothing but whoremen. And they were here on the depot platform to restock with female human flesh – just as cattlemen might attend a country fair to pick the 'American' breeds like Hereford, Devon and Angus that would improve a herd of Longhorns of Spanish or Mexican origin.

Their ribald jests covered cruel, calculating

natures. One of the men, with an Irish accent and small, red-rimmed eyes set close to a broken nose, stepped over to Kearny, sizing him up.

'Oi'm Finnegan, me bhoy. Seamus Finnegan,' he said. 'In from the railroaders' construction camp, where Oi got me the rip-roarin'est tent-town saloon in the whole South-West. Ye'll niver foind a loivelier, begorra! Sure, an' Oi wouldn't be pryin', but 'tis wonderin' we was – will ye be doin' business when the train comes in?'

Kearny didn't want to have truck with Finnegan or any of his circle. He took an instant dislike to his brash manner, to even his duds. The saloonman was decked out in a stretched suit with shiny wear marks and a string tie. He was a fat gent with broad hips, a massive gut and pudgy hands sporting two large rings. One was set with a showy bloodstone; the other was a signet-ring.

'For a feller who ain't prying, you're damn inquisitive,' Kearny said. 'I'm meeting folks, is all.'

'Is that so? *Wimmin* folks, Oi'll be bound! When Oi was your age an' no more'n a broth of a boy, Oi thought of not a thing at all but the colleens an' the hard stuff.'

Just whom Kearny might be meeting was

now part of his uneasiness. Kearny had never felt totally confident about the scheme cooked up by Sturman and Reece and apparently swallowed hook, line and sinker by the burghers of Rawhide Fork. But it had been hard to put a finger on his problem with it. After all, the outward chivalry of the West insisted that all women were wonderful. Associating himself with the venture was out of his ordinary line of work, but it wouldn't discredit him, surely?

Women did the cooking, the cleaning, the sewing. They were the real home-makers, obliging honest men to take a pride in themselves. They bore children and insisted on the orderly existence that made the rearing of them possible. Orderliness denoted progress.

Reece's argument – that women brought civilization and were sorely needed by the rugged frontier territories – had been incontestable.

Many a hell-raising tumbleweed, happy with a trusty bronc, a saddle and a blanket, had succumbed to the witchery of a woman's comforts.

But as Finnegan's type was proof, the West also knew women of a different stamp and the wholesale trafficking in them was a badly kept secret.

These other women were launched into their ages-old trade as young and pretty recruits, maybe paraded through plushy, mirrored bordellos in the sophistication of St Louis or San Francisco. Yet they were as often on their backs as their feet, and the profits from their body-sapping endeavours were forever creamed off by vice lords and madams. Quickly faded, cut off by their pimps to make way for fresher blooms, they slid down the line to insalubrious accommodations in the trail towns and mining and railroad camps where men could not be choosy.

Kearny might guess at the type of girls Finnegan and his coarse rivals were expecting the train to deliver, presumably in fulfilment of a prior order. At worst, the girls would be tainted with the corruption of their abdicated seducers, without morals or scruples. At best, they might include the naïve, lured West by promises of 'domestic service' in some hotel or private family at better wages than they could earn in their home towns, but lined up for rapid coercion into debauchery.

Finnegan closed one eye in a wink. 'Oi'll be bettin' some sly-fingered beauty is awarmin' your bed tonight. No cuddly piece would be givin' the refusal to a well set-up kiddo like ye. Now Oi'm thinkin' us two moight pool our efforts, ye lookin' an up-standin' gentlemen of foine, discriminatin' taste–'

'God forbid!' Kearny said tersely.

Unsettled by his conjecturing and irked by Finnegan's approach, Kearny turned his back on the Irishman, who snorted derisively. 'Huh, sure 'tis an acid-tongued cuss ye are, bejasus!'

Kearny moved off down the platform where he casually removed his Stetson. An envelope was tucked behind the hat's sweatband. Inside this envelope, Reece had told him, were his credentials. On the outside, in Reece's copperplate hand, was written 'Miss Temperance Doe'.

Kearny quietly read the name aloud to himself. It had a sober, reassuring ring. Miss Doe was one of the party of six he was to meet.

She'd been commissioned to assemble the group and supervise its railroad journey to Santa Fe. Moreover, he was given to understand the arriving women had been carefully selected from responses to notices placed by Rawhide Fork in the East's most respected journals.

Miss Doe would be recognizable by a pink-dyed ostrich feather in a black hat. Kearny wouldn't have to mingle with Finnegan and friends.

Which was as well, since he anticipated some unsavoury dickerings.

Besides checking out that their order for new blood had been properly filled, Kearny didn't doubt each of the whoremen would be minding the interests of his own enterprise and trying to pick perceived plums.

The incoming passenger train rumbled down the main track through the freight yard, smoke drifting lazily from the engine's big diamond stack. The engineer blew a single short toot of the whistle and it came to a brake-grinding, steam-hissing halt. The string of varnished, link-and-pin coupled cars clanked together alongside the platform.

Doors swung open. A Mexican porter climbed aboard the baggage car and began heaving off carpetbags and trunks. Passengers stepped down. First off were a trio of fat city men and their yammering wives; a youthful cowpoke encumbered with a saddle and bedroll; a lean, ascetic reverend father toting only a leather-bound Bible that bulged with inserted papers.

But Kearny's and the whoremongers' eyes were peeled for groups of females.

'Begorra! They'se all here. Genuine white women – sixteen, seventeen of 'em, me bhoys,' Finnegan announced, after striding the length of the train, looking in at the windows.

Kearny studied the disembarking women in tight-lipped silence. As he'd feared, a hard-eyed, middle-aged procuress shepherded most of the chattering girls into the ring formed by Finnegan and his peers. He felt sickened to see that of these eleven girls maybe all except two or three of the older ones were blushing innocents clearly un-aware of what lay in store for them.

He wondered what romantic notions had been put into their unsophisticated heads, and how long it would be before they were made aware that they were stranded friend-less in a strange town, there to be re-educated in the arts of a new profession: smoking, drinking, roping the male suckers, opening their soft white legs in upstairs rooms.

First, the empty chatter would turn into the plaintive panting and crying of cruelly ravished girls. But in a matter of weeks that also would give way – to the artful compliments and simulations of fallen women. Their formerly tear-filled eyes would be hard and knowing, smouldering...

Some among them, the true survivors, would find the enjoyment to be had in their new calling. They would take to it as though they'd been born for it alone.

Kearny didn't find this wholly depressing. Such ladies had a place along the trails of the West. A few among the most intelligent might even graduate to running their own parlour houses in the bigger towns and secure their own circles of admirers as they promoted the open and boisterous trade in well-developed tits and asses.

Kearny pushed the picture away from him, irritated that it should have formed there unbidden, but at the same time recognizing it was the kind of human frailty that allowed Finnegan and his ring to prosper while condemning babes to become trollops.

He would have liked to butt in and put the skids under the whoremen's game, but he had his own fish to fry. He looked around for his charges; for a pink plume in a black hat. And there it was among the stragglers emerging from the rear car.

As a party, the six young women lacked the simpering eagerness of the larger group already spoken for. Like Kearny had expected, they didn't make the same foolish noise, for which he was thankful. Like he'd not expected, the reason for this wasn't that they were refined gentlewomen in reduced circumstances; it was that they were of a breed actually more deserving of the whoremen's attentions.

Kearny blinked at them, dumbfounded. The paint on their pasty faces, their dress and most of all their demeanour marked them as ladies of the night. Hell, they were nothing but god-damned, dollar-a-throw chippies if he ever saw the like.

Miss Temperance Doe of the pink feather had blonde ringlets busting out from under the black hat. The blonde-ness was of the kind that came from a bottle of peroxide; the ringlets were curler-made. She carried the coat of a mustard travelling outfit over her arm and full breasts were also doing their best at busting out from a blouse of white silk that had long since taken on a tinge of yellowish grey.

'There should be a man waiting for us, girls,' she said.

'Ain't there always,' another woman with

hennaed hair said cynically, and her companions briefly tittered.

Knowing and vaguely shopworn, the women stepped onto this new ground with the wariness of cats venturing onto foreign territory. Not for them the bright hopes of the larger party of girls, nor the silly, empty talk. They were willing 'sports' here for the pickings.

Kearny's distrust of the Sturman-Reece project to improve Rawhide Fork deepened. According to the lawyer, each woman's background had been investigated. Sturman had cracked the whip and submissive towners, like Martinez and Mallison, had poured their money into the female immigrant scheme. Kearny doubted the rich cattleman had used a cent of his own to finance the mad dream.

Aside from the paying of the women's travel costs and his own hire, Kearny saw little evidence in the bunch before him of other expenditure, even of common sense. He wondered what kind of advertisements had really been placed and where. Maybe Sturman and Reece were holding a goodly balance of the small people's *dinero* in their personal accounts.

These might be women struck by misfortune and need. But they'd come up with their own ages-old answer, and it had hardened and coarsened them.

Kearny shrugged. It wasn't his money. His job was just to make sure this jaded bevy safely reached Rawhide Fork and collect payment for the chore.

10

'FIGHT, FIGHT!'

He went up, doffing his Stetson and holding out his letter to Temperance Doe. 'Howdy, ladies. I'm Will Kearny, come from Rawhide Fork to see to your transport.'

Kearny smiled and Temperance, whose head reached his shoulder, made a passable fist of sizing him up. The smile made the man look boyish but also set off the rugged strength in his square-chinned face and the rock-steady expression of confidence in his eyes. The tinge of grey in his hair gave him maturity. The gesture with his hat wafted the scent of barbershop toilet-water. 'Well, you look a straight shooter, cowboy. Tell you one thing – you can come an' transport me anytime you like.'

She batted blacked lashes at him roguishly, thrust her uplifted bosom and swayed her wide, firm hips.

Now Kearny was closer, he saw she had a mole on one cheek of her hard face and wore on ears and fingers a quantity of flashy, fake jewellery with stones that looked like chips of coloured glass. Her mouth was a mite too large, but this could have been the result of the way she'd painted her lips. The folks who'd named her Temperance some twenty-five years back had to have made the biggest unintentional joke of their lives.

'Don't even need washing first, does he, Temperance?' said a sturdy member of her troupe, underlining the bawdy nature of her invitation.

To Kearny's annoyance, the exchange was not going unobserved.

Seamus Finnegan came bustling over. 'Now look ye here, me bhoy. Let not hasty words come between us gentlemen. To be sure an' it's not too late to talk turkey indeed, indeed.' His buzzard eyes appraised the women bound for Rawhide Fork. 'Ye got the proper goods here an' no mistake. Oi'll not be a-needin' those not even green-broke.'

He waved a fat-fingered hand dismissively in the direction of the other arrivals. 'A pretty passel o' raw novices, yet 'twould be a tearful month with fits and faintin's afore the useless ones was weeded out. Oi could not bear the foolishness.

'On t'other hand, your friends here would be the better suitin' me customers, to be sure. Workin' women for workin' men. A tired steel-drivin' man deserves to be gettin' his comforts reliable an' fast – from by-the-hour women who know the ropes an' do their craft with no childish spats. Nothin' too fragile nor bony-shanked, ye'll be appreciatin'.'

Kearny glowered. 'I think you've said enough. These ladies are heading for honest positions in a decent community.'

Finnegan laughed at him. 'Ye must be more fool-blind than ye look!'

He reached out a paw to grasp the wrist of the woman nearest him and pulled her toward him. 'Niver lissen to this driveller, me darlin',' he wheedled. 'Ye need travel no farther. Oi've friends hereabouts who'll be a-rarin' to go to bat for ye an' your spunky sisters. Jest come with me.'

Surprisingly, Kearny saw the girl he'd accosted flinch and try to shake his hand free. 'No, sir!' she objected. 'You're mistaken. I *want* to go to Rawhide Fork.'

Kearny's undivided attention was drawn for the first time to the woman Finnegan had picked on. He noted that she was by fluke the one showing the least professional interest in his blandishments.

Maybe that was because she also looked the least likely to fit Finnegan's criteria for a robust entertainer of muscular railroad workers. She was younger and thinner than the others, something of a lost lamb among a pack of wolf bitches. The appealing swells of first womanhood were shamed by the tightly immodest fit of her faded floral dress and her slim hand not captured by Finnegan was clutching a cheap paper suitcase.

Most strikingly, she was topped by a cloud of dark hair. Seemingly, all the energy in her growth had been diverted from her slender frame into sustaining the vital abundance of her frizzy locks.

Her fragility and defencelessness struck Kearny acutely. He suddenly suspected the rouge and powder on her finely boned face disguised not the ravages of harlotry but the unlikely bloom of youth. A quality of beauty and delicacy came through. She also had the prettiest eyes, a deep violet-blue, and a look about them that seemed strangely familiar.

'You heard, Finnegan,' he said sharply. 'Leave the girl go and hightail it.'

Temperance flung him a reckless glare.

'Aw, hell, let's not get on high horses. Chrissie is tired, is all. Maybe we could work in taking up some of this gent's offer along the way. Besides, we ain't leaving this here Santa Fe till morning an' all-night fetches more'n ten dollars in most any neck of the woods.'

Kearny noticed the tension gather in the drawn features of the girl Temperance Doe called Chrissie, the look of apprehension that sprang into her grave eyes.

'Ain't nothing like that in my instructions, Miss Doe,' he curtly told the brash spokeswoman. 'Now, Finnegan, hoof it someplace else!'

But Irish-born nature being what it was, it was going to take more than orders from a lone stranger to budge Finnegan.

'Oi will not! Oi say ye's a bucko out to hog all the fun for hisself and Oi'm hornin' in an' stickin'.'

As a range boss, Kearny had been a bender of men to his purpose. He'd taken in the lessons of toughness and determination, and learned to calculate the moments when the need was to bring things to a head with physical action.

He got a grip on Finnegan's shoulder, spun him round and chopped down on his forearm. This freed his grip on the nervous girl, who staggered back a step or two with a small cry.

Finnegan roared, 'Ye'll not manhandle me, ye mealy-mouthed spalpeen!' His beady eyes blazed with hatred and he promptly balled a beringed fist and swung it.

Kearny was ready and ducked the hot-tempered punch that would have knocked the daylights out of him had it landed.

He had no illusions about his opponent. Finnegan was a big, heavy-set man. He followed the railroad builders, mixing it with and taking profits from some of the rowdiest and meanest men the West had known. To run a business like his and survive, Finnegan had to be a seasoned rough-house fighter.

Kearny tackled the job like practising a science. He straightened up and jabbed a quick response at Finnegan's head before he could regain balance from his wild swing.

The blow connected with the side of the whoreman's skull. It was like hitting rock.

Finnegan backed off, snarling, putting up his guard.

Temperance Doe said from the edge of the gathering ring of spectators, 'Hell, you'll have to do better than that, cowboy!'

Somebody started yelling, 'Fight! Fight!'

The girl called Chrissie cried, 'Do stop it, please!'

The two men came together again violently. A ponderous, right-handed blow grazed Kearny's cheekbone, the bloodstone ring scraping skin. It was dizzying enough to warn him that a full-on hit would be a bone-cracker, a fight-finisher. He swayed away from Finnegan's following left, but managed to stab a power-packed punch of his own into the misshapen nose, which he judged had seen previous injury and was a possible weak point.

Kearny was rewarded. Blood bubbled from the right nostril. Men growled; a girl squealed, more out of excitement than fright. *'He's bleeding!'*

Finnegan swiped the blood away with the back of his hand. 'Oi'll wallop ye, bucko!' he slurred.

He windmilled in, beringed fists flailing. Kearny was forced to retreat to the irritation of Temperance and her friends. 'Quit pussy-footing around, cowboy!' she called.

'I ain't,' Kearny said under his breath. Finnegan wasn't stopped by his rebroken nose, so he'd have to try something else.

Kearny figured Finnegan was carrying too much weight around the mid-section to go any distance. A second weak point! He tucked down his head and bored in fast, oblivious to punishment, pummelling at Finnegan's gut.

His fists buried themselves to the wrist.

The breath belched gustily out of Finnegan's mouth and he couldn't replace it fast enough. The force left his chopping fists. He was put down on the seat of his pants, his bloodied face purpling.

The crowd sighed, seeing this as a terminal development.

Kearny grabbed Finnegan by his string tie and a bunch of his shirtfront and hauled him to his feet.

The man stood unsteadily, still retching. Kearny immediately decked him again, this time with a punch he brought up from the ground and that caught Finnegan squarely under the bracket of his jaw.

Finnegan was lifted off his feet and went down flat, as though struck by a club. He didn't sit up.

'Oooh!' said Temperance, ogling the victor. 'I do admire to be with a strong man.'

Kearny stepped back, rubbing his knuckles. 'All right, Miss Doe. Let's leave it at that. I reckon we've drawn enough attention. C'mon.'

He took her by the arm and hastily propelled her away from the buzzing scene. The rest of her troupe followed unquestioningly.

Kearny noticed the girl Finnegan had accosted was white-faced, and her eyes as grave as ever, filled with a sad resignation. Where had he seen that expression previously? It bothered him as much as anything else about this bizarre set-up: the vague feeling that their tracks must have crossed before.

He knew that it wasn't so, but he couldn't pin it down and he couldn't ignore it. It was like some half-remembered range tune that kept jangling through your head with ditty and title just out of reach.

Kearny stood before the open window of the Santa Fe hotel's dining-room, listening to the tinkling of a cheap piano from a neighbouring building, staring out at the narrow, crooked street. A freight wagon lumbered by on its way out of town, laden with goods for the railroad builders' camps that were just over the surrounding small hills. It carried picks and shovels, bags of oats and bales of hay.

The more Kearny thought about bringing his charges from Santa Fe to Rawhide Fork, the greater his unease became.

He couldn't rightly figure what purpose Sturman and Reece could have in foisting the women on the town, nor how the women themselves could hope to begin lives afresh as prospective wives in a rural backwater; whether, in fact, they would want to. Without considerable changes to their get-up and outlook, their chances of marriage were damned awful slim.

The slender girl with the magnificent hair – whose full name, he'd learned, was Miss Christine Smith – appeared at his elbow. She mightn't be alluring, but she was good-looking in a way Kearny liked.

She had a fine face, kind, thoughtful and, above all, brave.

'I wanted to thank you, Mr Kearny,' she said quietly. 'I'm under no illusions about the company I've placed myself in. To that Irishman we must've appeared – available. I'm sorry you were obliged to fight on my behalf.'

Kearny returned her steady gaze musingly. 'No matter what he thought, Miss Smith, he laid hands on you without say-so, which ain't right, howsoever a woman might look. Besides, the fight came out of the job I've hired on to do.'

'An unlooked-for part, surely?'

'But part of it just the same. There's no thanks due from you.' Again, he took in her youth and hidden freshness, and wondered. He shook his head. 'Miss Smith, aside from what's already arisen, I smell trouble aplenty. If I may make a personal observation, I think you're making a mistake, getting involved. You've fallen in with a rough crowd here, one where I don't reckon you rightly belong. Maybe you should buy yourself a railroad ticket to ride back East *pronto*.'

The girl looked flustered by his concerned commentary. She gave a flap of her thin arms like a bird learning to fly.

'But that's not possible, Mr Kearny. You see, I don't immediately have the money, and I don't see how a young woman could quickly earn it.'

The refreshing openness of her answer merely confirmed Kearny's suspicions. 'You don't?' he said.

Understanding left her groping for words. 'Oh ... oh, yes, of course,' she said in confusion, realizing the naïvety of what she'd said and reddening. 'Miss Doe could – er – arrange an introduction for me, I'm sure. Santa Fe is a very bustling place.'

The unseen pianist had launched into a new number, the tinny notes accompanying a woman singing something in Spanish too unutterably mournful and sentimental for any other tongue.

Kearny thought of the land speculators, gamblers and drunken riff-raff they'd seen thronging the sidewalks about the plaza and reached a quixotic decision.

'That wouldn't be necessary.' He delved into his pocket and peeled off bills from the roll given him by Reece. 'Here, I ain't got much, but you're welcome.'

The girl shook her head vehemently. 'I couldn't do that.'

'If you like, when you get back to New York and can afford it, you could mail it me, care of the post office at Rawhide Fork.'

'No, no! In all honesty, I've no desire to return to New York. Though purportedly the cultural capital, it's a hateful place, full of poseurs and scoundrels.'

Kearny looked at her disbelievingly, but she appeared quite adamant.

Her voice, though still light, took on great intensity. 'In the city, life is mean and cruel for the less fortunate. The conventions of civilization mask foulness you wouldn't credit. I've the strongest desire to go to Rawhide Fork. In fact, I leaped at the amazing chance.'

'A chance to live in a cow town?'

She waved her small hands, dismissing his puzzled enquiry. 'You're right, I'm not like the other girls with us. They're creatures of the cities. I've lived on the frontier before – when I was yet a child, it's true – but I've some idea of what it offers.'

Kearny rubbed his clean-shaven jaw. The information she poured out surprised him. But for some reason he didn't think or care to explore, he was glad she'd refused the money anyway, and he stuffed it back into his pocket.

'Well, it's a free country, I guess. But I hope you do have some idea of what you're letting yourself in for. Why, I don't even know myself anymore what that might rightly be.'

What Kearny did know was that in giving up the attempt to persuade her to turn back he'd committed himself to something that seemed a sight more meaningful to him than his responsibility to escort the party safely to Rawhide Fork, four days away. In his soft heart, he'd taken on the job of being the enigmatic Christine Smith's special protector.

The girl gave him a wan smile. 'Thank you again, Mr Kearny. I'll be going to my room now. Coach travel's very fatiguing as I remember, and the rest we had on the train wasn't the best. I'll bid you goodnight.'

He watched her cross the room to the narrow stairs. She gathered her skirt and mounted them, her fluid movements artlessly sensuous.

Temperance Doe appeared from the shadows on the upper landing. He wondered how long she'd been there, how much she'd heard of their quiet conversation.

It was like a cat with a mouse. 'To bed so early, Chrissie?' Temperance said. 'My, it'll grow you into a proper beauty yet.'

Christine Smith laughed nervously and squeezed past her. 'It's time a little girl ran along.'

Temperance sailed up to Kearny with a lopsided grin. 'God, that one won't ever make it, will she? I saw her turn down your greenbacks, cowboy. Getting real choosy, our Chrissie. She's a good bit of bait, but I'll have to let her know the score before we get to Rawhide Fork.'

Kearny wagged his head. 'I think you misunderstood what you saw, Miss Doe.'

She gave a peal of laughter. 'Aw, you're stiff in all the wrong places, cowboy. Don't be put out by it. She turns down most of the guys that hanker to lay her. Can't understand it. You'd think she didn't know what a feller itches to do to a gal who takes his fancy.'

'Maybe she doesn't,' Kearny said flatly.

Temperance laughed again, but it was more of a scoff. 'Take it from Temperance – she's been done over, an' proper. Just workshy an' cussed, I'd say. You can see she don't eat enough, an' no wonder.'

The conversation troubled Kearny. He couldn't define it; notwithstanding, it made a churning sensation behind his belt. 'Maybe some shuteye would do us all good, Miss Doe.'

'For Cris-sakes! Call me Temperance, will you, an' loosen up. As for bed, we girls've been given a four-poster in each room. There's plenty of room in 'em, an' I'm out on this free-spending town to see if any gentlemen care to come an' keep us company.'

11

JUSSERAND'S DEADLY CHORE

Arch Leggat was at the café across from the First Claim sipping breakfast coffee, bitter and black, when he saw Seabury Reece duck down the dog-trot that separated the saloon from a harness shop.

Leggat was a range man. His thinking ran along basic lines and was seldom deep, though it was often shrewd in the way of nature's open-air creatures, of whom he was one.

The events concerning the Rocking T and Will Kearny's departure for Santa Fe had him flummoxed. But he knew if he waited and watched closely, his curiosity might be answered. This was the invariable law of the wild and Leggat was content to follow it.

The evening before, giving no notice, Seth Mallison had abruptly closed the First Claim for 'renovations' which had quickly become a subject of town gossip.

Now lawyer Reece, who was tied in with

the other matters puzzling Leggat, was making what looked like a furtive, early-morning call at the premises, because the dog-trot gave on to the alley behind the saloon, where Mallison had a private back door to his quarters and office.

Leggat was interested. He set his hat on his head, pawed deep in a pocket and dumped some coins atop the counter. Venturing forth into the pleasant post-dawn chill of the day, he hobbled hurriedly across the empty roadway.

Swift moving was something he usually did on the back of a horse, but he slipped into the dog-trot with a haste moderated only by the caution to prevent the metallic whisper of spur rowels.

Reece was out of sight, which meant he must have been let in by the back door. Leggat hunkered down behind a trash barrel under an open window and strained his ears.

Mallison was complaining. 'Yeah, Reece, the layouts for the games are in these boxes, but I've only got one pair of hands. We'll set up the tables soon as all the painting's done. I got pails of the stuff to slap on.'

Reece's voice said, 'Mr Sturman is sending two of his crew to lend a hand with the chores. How about the upstairs rooms off the gallery? Have you got beds in each one?'

'Hell ... 'course I have,' Mallison said indignantly. 'Mirrors yet in some. I ain't stupid. I savvy what you want. Can't supply the doves though.'

'You know how that's being done.'

'Mayor Martinez'll be apt to blow his top when he sees how you fixed it using the public revenues.'

'You'll keep him sweet, Mallison – and his no-hoper council. Remember, all the blame for the kind of women brung in gets loaded onto Kearny. Mr Sturman's hands stay clean. Put a foot wrong and we'll call in the loan you got on this little goldmine.'

Much of the pair's talk went over Leggat's head, but he was absorbed, getting the drift and not liking it, when newcomers to the alley jumped him.

'Mister, you come out of there awful slow an' careful!'

Before that there hadn't been a word, not a blessed sound from the two range men who now menaced him with drawn six-guns. Leggat recognized them as Baldy Hogsden and another Arrowhead rider.

'Your goose is cooked,' Hogsden went on with a sneer. 'Our boss don't like rannies who sneak around an' listen at windows, an' this time it's us who's got the drop on you. Yuh'll get paid back fer sure. Reach around left-handed an' drop your belt gun!'

Hogsden's companion went in by the saloon's back door and summoned Seabury Reece.

The lawyer's face was dark with anger. 'Get him away from town before the place opens up. We don't know how much he's heard and can't afford to have him flapping his mouth.'

'But we just got here, Mr Reece. Sent to paint,' the Arrowhead rider said, somewhat disgruntled.

Reece was flustered but adamant. 'This takes priority. Sturman will have to decide what he wants done. Take him out to Arrowhead headquarters.'

Leggat knew he was up against a couple of snakes, waiting for a chance to strike. If he started anything, it would turn into a bloody scrimmage – and most of the blood would be his. He was tied in the saddle of his own mount, fetched from the livery barn, and Hogsden and his grumbling sidekick retraced their ride across the range's sweep of grass and sage to Sturman's home lot.

Franz Sturman's sprawling *hacienda* had a

bright red tile roof visible for miles. They arrived in the silent air of mid-morning.

Sturman was in his big office facing onto the yard and peppertree-lined trail back of the residence. The rich and powerful cowman was no more pleased than his Rawhide Fork attorney.

'I see the point, boys, but prisoners are an embarrassment,' he told his riders, drawing on a pungent cigar. At Leggat, he glowered. 'You got anything to say, feller?'

'Naw. 'Cept I'm bein' held outside o' the law.'

Hogsden laughed like a hyena. 'Mr Sturman is the law around here. Amos Gurney got his marchin' orders an' had the brains to foller 'em. So what are yuh gonna do about it?' He waved his six-gun around Leggat's head as though he was about to pistol-whip him.

'Nothin'. Who in hell wants to get his skull cracked or maybe half an ear torn off?'

Sturman grinned. 'Very sensible... Boys, this Rocking T deadbeat kinda galls me. Put him out of sight till we come up with an idea what to do with him. There's that Messican curing shed on what used to be the Esteven place.'

Leggat knew the old Esteven hundred

acres, a holding long since swallowed up by Arrowhead expansion. He thought he remembered the shed specified – an adobe structure, its mud walls fortress thick, its solid timber door secured by a massive *tranca*, or bar, hung across it in iron brackets.

His spirits sank, and the two hardcases hustled him out with no more ado. His nut-brown face was paled to the colour of clay.

After they'd gone, Sturman returned to the ledger open on his desk, but behind his calculating eyes his thoughts were elsewhere. Nor was it long before his office door was rapped again.

Bull Jusserand lumbered in, battered sombrero in his huge fists.

Sturman knew without asking more trouble was in the air.

'Yeah, what is it?' Sturman barked.

Jusserand was cruel and stupid, but he was as loyal as a dog to its man. And slow though his mind was, once an idea had been fixed in it, his massive physical power could be relied on to put it into crushing execution. He shuffled onto the bear hide that covered part of the varnished floor. The tale had it that Sturman had personally slaughtered the grizzly in hand-to-paw combat in the Sierras. Jusserand turned his hat in his hands.

144

'That ol' bastard Thwaites. He ain't bin run out o' the country yet.'

'How's that, Bull?'

'I seen him when I was out ridin' the high pasture. Reck'n he's made camp in the old Navajo's Cave in the foothills. I follered him some way, but he was smart an' lay up in ambush. He had a big ol' Sharps buffalo gun an' warned me off.'

Sturman scowled. 'Damn it. These Rocking T snoopers are getting in my hair.'

Bull's gaze shifted from his boss's face to his head. 'Huh? They messed with your hair?'

'Just a manner of speaking, Bull.' Sturman kept his patience. 'Let me *think*...'

After a while, the tight muscles in Sturman's hard face relaxed. 'Yeah. We'll settle it this way.' He leaned forward and gave Jusserand his instructions in simple language that couldn't be misconstrued.

Later, Jusserand rode off alone to Esteven's disused curing shed to do his work. He took Leggat's bronc on a lead rein.

Even the adobe's three-foot thick walls could not completely muffle Arch Leggat's screams. Birds broke squawking from the tall bunches of porcupine grass that grew round about.

145

In the semi-darkness and out of the full heat of the afternoon, Jusserand pummelled Leggat. With fists and boots, he smashed bones and deformed flesh like a mad butcher tenderizing a slab of meat.

That was the part of his chore Jusserand most enjoyed. But he still had the rest of his orders to carry out.

Will Kearny frowned. Temperance Doe's avowed intention to solicit on the night-time streets of Santa Fe filled him with disquiet. The go-round with Finnegan at the Lamy railroad depot had been enough for one day. He didn't relish a clash with the hotel management, nor having to throw out the 'company' Temperance might entice if its appetites led to riotous demands.

'I wouldn't do that, Temperance. This town's changing now the railroad's opening up the territory. There's dirty drunks and desperadoes of every stripe out there.'

Temperance pouted. 'Well, we can't help that, can we? A girl has to make a living.' She turned for the door with a flounce.

Kearny caught her shoulder. 'Wait a minute. How much do you need to stay right here where I can keep an eye on you?'

'You mean, in your room?' Temperance

probed coquettishly.

His voice became gruff. 'If that's what it takes.'

'Damn me, I got to admit you stack up han'some, cowboy. For you, ten dollars for all-night. Is that a bargain or isn't it?'

Kearny unstuck the words from inside his throat. 'All right. Done.'

'I sure expect to be,' she said, smiling broadly. 'Let's hop to it up those stairs.'

They went up to Kearny's room next to the three shared by the girls on the third floor. 'Stuffy up here,' Temperance said, sitting on the bed and pulling off her shoes. 'Ain't you going to get out of your duds?'

Kearny put an eagle ten-dollar gold piece on the dresser beside the water pitcher and washbowl. He didn't offer any reply to Temperance's question, but said, 'All night buys me the right to ask what I like, don't it?'

'Yep. Chrissie got you worked up for it, didn't she? Then she dropped you flat when you showed the colour of your money. Where the hell's her manners?'

'Miss Smith's manners suit me fine.'

Temperance paused in shucking her blouse. He wasn't starting to shed so much as a boot. She had large breasts that stood out with none of the sagging common in the well-endowed. She was disappointed that he showed no reaction.

'Hey, ain't you going to do anything, cowboy? If you need a bootjack, I've got a Naughty Lady in my room.'

'For openers, I'm asking questions. About Miss Smith.'

Temperance said disgustedly, 'God, that girl must've put blinkers on you! Forget it for now. We're wasting your bought time. She was stupid to turn you down. Maybe I been stupid, too, having her along.'

'Why did you?'

'Because she was the keenest that answered the advertisements in New York an' a real head-turner. I ain't much older than her, cowboy, but I've been down the line before, to Kansas City and Abilene. I've seen what men like.'

Kearny pondered that. 'She don't behave like your other girls. How can you reckon she belongs? She's not much more'n a child.'

Temperance clucked her tongue, exasperated. 'Look, mister, I'll be honest. I did fret about her capabilities. I wasn't recruiting innocents. God knows there's thousands in the game between here an' San Francisco who're going to die by violence, disease or in a poorhouse. Some will even do themselves in with laudanum.'

'You didn't succeed in dissuading her,' Kearny accused.

Temperance rolled her eyes. 'Believe me, I told her straight. But she said she wasn't a faint-heart. She could take it, an' what's more she fitted all the requirements listed in the newspaper. Her mama had died, she'd no kinfolks in New York an' she was at the bottom of the barrel financially. She'd already been forced to discard the conceits of a repressed upbringing – her virginity, for starters.'

'Mightn't she have been falsifying?'

'What about? The men? She assured me she had acquaintance with what pleasured 'em. Best I could do was get her to confess she was abstaining while she could. I said don't spare yourself for too long, dearie, or you might lose the touch.'

'Damn it! It seems wrong you didn't turn her away.'

'She badgered me to take her in an' give her the chance to show she'd be no scrounger.'

Temperance squirmed under Kearny's critical but enquiring gaze. She licked her red lips and went on, 'Despite her claims, it came out little by little that she hadn't done so very much. She was anxious to be educated by me an' the other girls. But I liked that. There's nothing worse than a know-all. She said she'd go as far as any woman, so I gave her an album of French photographs. They fascinated her.'

Kearny was puzzled. 'She wants to travel to Europe?'

Temperance forgot her discomfiture; his question brought salacious merriment bubbling from her lips. 'They were pictures taken in a Paris salon – of saucy courtesans with pumpkin bosoms an' pear-shaped bottoms pleasing brawny patrons in positions no ordinary American girl would dream of.'

'Oh.'

'Chrissie was some surprised. Mind you, there was one page she seemed to pause over regular, kinda thoughtful. It started with a *cocotte* on hands an' knees, dipping her back an' presenting her ass to the camera. The picturetaker must've gotten plenty stewed up under his lightcloth. The last print in the set showed the girl getting her mischief's deservings from a truly Olympian stud.'

'There's no good reason for a young woman to be shown things like that,' Kearny growled.

'Phooey!' said Temperance. 'She was familiar with what was going on in those pictures for sure.'

'Miss Smith's a born lady, I swear. Her reserve makes the truth of your story hard to accept,' he said.

Temperance was stung. 'I'm telling you no lies! Don't be misled by Chrissie's youthful looks.'

'I hope she can be let to keep her youth.'

'She needn't waste it. Profitable chances wait out West for our Miss Smith. Gents'll let her name a top price.'

'Maybe we've talked enough about this,' Kearny said through his teeth.

But Temperance blabbed on. 'Well that, cowboy, is the sum of it. Sweet Chrissie's delicacy survives only in the imaginations of deluded fools. She's just another working girl an' unless she backslides permanently she's got better prospects than many.'

Temperance's blunt and bawdy talk was getting to Kearny. He realized he was slick with sweat and deeply unsettled.

'Obliged for the information,' he said bitterly.

12

NOISES IN THE NIGHT

Christine Smith's room-mate was a round-faced, buxom brunette known not long since to the bravos and courts of New York as Black-eyed Sadie. She'd pinned up her hair, shadowed her eyelids with kohl and was putting crimson on her lips at the cracked and flecked mirror over the washstand.

'So there you are,' she said, when Christine entered their room. 'I thought you'd gone out on the town without me.'

'Mr Kearny says it's not safe. I'm not going out anywhere.'

'Temperance has.'

'Unless Mr Kearny stopped her. But I can't anyway. We mightn't be good girls, but our word should still be good, and I told Mr Kearny I was going to bed.'

Christine considered Sadie's preparations. 'Actually, I'm sure you must be tired, too.'

Sadie thought about it, then dropped her warpaint and straightened up from the mirror with a loud sigh of resignation.

'All right... All right, Chrissie dear. Anyway, I can hardly bring someone back here less'n you're game to work as well, can I?'

'You think not?'

'Silly girl! No hot-blood that saw a dainty dish like you in the bed would want to do anything but try two on the trot. Men are such greedy shit-asses....'

Christine gulped, grateful for Sadie's consideration. 'I'll try to repay your kindness another time.'

What her mother had referred to darkly as fornication had become part of the concessionary way of life she'd been forced to embrace in New York. The choice was basic, stark and simple: a strong-backed, homeless girl with no means of support would as soon rent out her body as let it starve and sicken.

To this reality she was now more or less inured, never mind that it might make her a 'brazen hussy' according to the supposedly decent principles instilled by Mama.

But she appreciated that Sadie did not want to begrudge her a respite in Santa Fe.

The girls disrobed, Christine washed her face, blew out the lamp and they retired to their bed, a double four-poster.

'Aw, shake out of it, can't you, cowboy?' Temperance pleaded. 'In truth, I haven't let anything happen to Chrissie Smith she didn't ask for. What's more, you've got me here an' paid for. We can do better than chew the rag.'

Kearny struggled to curb the tide of bitterness that had risen in him.

'Reckon she was owed a better chance. She's young and gracious; she shouldn't be turning herself into a two-bit tramp.'

What he said was tactless, given the circumstances he'd put himself in, but the pain in his voice alerted Temperance to his state of mind. Clients' double standards were nothing new to her. She took no personal offence and shrewdly changed the topic, hoping to distract him and maybe put him in better humour.

'How do you like that? There's one in every room.'

She indicated a framed text that hung on the wall over the bed's headboard. The ornamental script proclaimed, *'With God all things are possible. Matthew, xix, 26.'*

Kearny shrugged. 'Some folk set a lot of store by their Bible.'

'I don't have much truck with preaching, but on second thoughts, I can live with that,'

Temperance said. 'Specially where it's put.' The comment was delivered with careful inflection and a wry smile.

The cramped room had no chair, so Kearny sat himself on the edge of the bed to tug off his boots. 'I don't think it was placed with carnal transactions in mind,' he said.

Temperance laughed lightly. 'The bellhop told me the hotel's part of the holdings of a railroad financier called Halliday. He insists on such trimmings apparently. He's very pious an' contributes hugely to foreign missions and Bible societies.'

'If you knew the type of men who probably do Mr Halliday's railroad empire-building, you'd realize there was consider-able hypocrisy in that,' Kearny said. 'And I know he won't succeed in foisting his piety on his hotel's present guests.'

Temperance stood up and trailed her fingers across his shoulders. 'If that's the case, what's the point in not passing our time less boringly?' The fingers crept over to his chest and deftly undid shirt buttons.

Temperance's touch was sure and profes-sional, teasing out the tightness from his tensed muscles. He surrendered to her attentions. Her breasts seemed bigger than ever as she leaned over, letting a hard nipple come close to brushing his cheek.

'Lie down, won't you?' she said.

'Temperance, huh!' he objected half-heartedly. 'Temptress, more like.'

'Nothing of the sort, cowboy. I don't cheat on anyone an' you're due your ten dollars' worth,' she reminded him.

Her hands forced him down gently onto the bed. He went without resistance, because he was weary of shouldering the burden of a niggling guilt he knew wasn't rightly his. He also knew she had the power to take him out of himself.

'Now we're getting somewhere,' she said.

Kearny watched her bend over the lamp, fussing with it.

'We'll turn down the lamp an' you can pretend I'm Chrissie,' she said. 'What's the difference in the dark?'

Kearny mentally swore at his transparency.

The lamp glass glowed the colour of old whiskey.

A little later, Temperance said, 'I'm glad you found your senses.'

The intensity of their pleasure quickly overcame fatigue, bringing mutual, wordless demand for immediate repetition till they were carried to sighing satiety. Finally, they fell asleep, still joined.

Christine went to sleep almost at once, despite the strange surroundings and her guilty thoughts. But it was a less than comfortable sleep. She dreamed of being chased through the dark streets of New York's Lower East Side by Eli Greenbaum and a burly captain of police. She was wearing nothing but a pair of crotchless, pink satin French drawers and the officer was crying 'Murderer!' and 'Whore!' in an Irish brogue. She turned at bay in a trash-strewn alley where the gas lamps flickered unreliably. A nickel-plated derringer in her hand went off with a double crack and her pursuers were suddenly both wearing drab green shirts with holes in them that fountained blood.

In her dream, the gun's bullets were ineffective. The policeman caught her, snarling Irish imprecations, and wrestled her onto a bed with screeching springs, and she was twisting and turning. And, all at once – awake!

The sheets were clinging to the dampness of her perspiration and her heart was thumping wildly in her breast. The Irish policeman became Seamus Finnegan. She identified him from the remembered grasp of his pudgy, beringed fingers and his broken-nosed profile silhouetted against the greyness of the thinly curtained window.

She tried to scream but his loathsome hand went over her mouth and she realized other men were in the room, too.

She heard Sadie's muffled cry, a thrashing about and the sound of rent clothing. A man gave a whistling grunt and a foul curse. 'Kneed me in the groin, the bitch!' he said.

'Shut up!' hissed another. 'Get 'em outa here an' yuh can pay her back betwixt *her* legs.'

'If'n I ain't damaged perm'nent, that is.'

Christine fought as though her life depended on it. She clawed at the hand over her mouth, feeling her fingernails tear as they snagged on a ring. Her own flimsy garments were ripped in her frenzied gyrations.

'Begorra, she's a spirited colleen, this 'un!' Finnegan lilted. 'Gimme the bottle an' rag, will ye? Hustle, me buckos!'

Someone swung across her the narrow shaft of light from a bull's-eye lantern with its metal slide half-shut. Shadows leaped on the walls huge and menacing. Men laughed, and she was in no doubt from the belly-deep tone she'd come to know that it was occasioned by her near-nudity.

More hands groped her, some with an

intent only tenuously linked to restraining her.

'Easy on that, easy!' Finnegan said. 'Ah, the fixings...'

The hand pressed against her bruised lips was taken away. She opened them to scream, but a dampened cloth was whisked over her mouth and she drew in not air but lungfuls of powerful, smothering vapours.

The lantern's light was swallowed up in all-enveloping blackness.

Kearny awoke to muffled sounds that came from outside the room, through the walls: a thump, a continuous creaking of tortured bedsprings, and low, urgent mumblings.

He pulled free and lifted himself onto an elbow. 'What's that?' he demanded.

Temperance snuggled herself up against him, her heavy breasts seductively warm against his bare back. 'Take it easy, cowboy. I'm paid for till morning, remember?'

'There's something going on in one the girls' rooms,' he said, the sleepiness falling away from him.

Sitting up, Temperance pushed a hand through her mussed-up ringlets. A smile quirked the smudgy outline of her lips.

'Sure. I ain't the only one who has to turn

her pennies. I 'spect some of the others went out an' brought in a bit of business. Lie down again, won't you?'

'Dammit, I thought they'd been told that wasn't wise,' Kearny said. He strained his ears and heard what sounded like dragging footsteps pass the door.

'There,' said Temperance. 'They're leaving directly. So you can let it go an' think about other things. Like something that's fallen out of its nest.'

Once Will Kearny had left the Rocking T, old Pete Thwaites hadn't lingered himself. He'd no reason not to light out. Legal papers had still to be signed at Seabury Reece's office, but Thwaites didn't fool himself. Once he'd abandoned his property, Arrowhead crew would simply ride over it at will and take possession. It had happened to others' land. No one was going to lose sleep over his absence, and Franz Sturman would be the first to say good riddance.

Yet in his stubborn way Thwaites was also intrigued to know why Sturman had gotten anxious to take over the mediocre parcel that made up the Rocking T. If he stayed around and kept his eyes peeled, maybe he would stumble on something.

161

Accordingly, Thwaites 'went Injun', transplanting himself, plus the needings to last out in back country to the high place known as the Navajo's Cave.

The cave was big and dry, warm at night and cool by day, with space in the back if necessary for his part-Kentucky black. Apart from the comfort it offered, the cave was also safe from attack or siege. Brush- and boulder-littered approaches would present alleys of covered escape if needed.

In nightfall's deepening shadows, Thwaites tended the cooking of his supper, sucking on his corn-cob pipe. The firehole was in black-ened rock by the partly masked entrance to the cave and was kept covered by dirt when not in use.

He was regretting the most significant event of his day, his near clash with the Arrowhead hulk, Louey 'Bull' Jusserand. Still, there was little he could do about that now.

'Bull ain't nothin' till closer than spittin' range. Sturman is smart as a circus monkey, but the smartest monkey aroun' ain't gonna flush me outa here,' he opined to himself owlishly.

His first warning that visitors were approaching his hideout was via the black, picketed on a long tether in a little meadow downslope apiece, full-fed but restless. The black lifted his drowsy head and whickered.

Thwaites put aside his pipe, shifted the holstered sixgun on his shellbelt and got to his feet, debating whether to go fetch the single-load Sharps .50-90 stashed in the cave.

Hoofs struck against loose rocks; another whicker answered the black's.

Thwaites placed the sounds in the narrow defile, the bed of a defunct stream, that wound up from the prairie. The makeshift trail was overhung by cottonwoods and oaks. Moreover, it was already in deep darkness. He could see nothing.

'Hullo, down thar'!' he challenged. 'Come on up real slow, whosoever yuh are!'

He drew his old Army Colt, not trusting a damn that the visit to his camp was friendly.

Thwaites judged two horses were negotiating the hidden incline, but after he called out they came to a halt. No one answered him, which was spooky enough, but then he heard a jingle of harness metal, a stamping of hoofs and the snapping of tree growth. He figured a horse was being turned around in the narrow space of the wash.

They'd bothered to come, but were they

going without confronting him?

It made no sense.

Thwack! A slap on horseflesh, a startled equine snort and a whinny of anger reached Thwaites's puzzled hearing.

The sounds were followed by a clatter of retreating hoofbeats that faded rapidly away down the wooded gully. Unless Thwaites missed his guess, however only one horse left.

He peered into the gloom. A horse – the one that had been slapped? – drifted on up the slope. He could hear its hard breathing.

If only it wasn't getting so plumb dark.

The approaching beast loomed into sight, a sorrel with a familiar gait and no rider.

'Arch...? Arch Leggat?' Thwaites called, recognizing the cayuse as his former hand's mount. He swept the brush with hard-eyed intensity but no man appeared.

Hearing his voice, the sorrel stopped short, seemingly reluctant to come the last ten yards. It kept lifting its hoofs on the spot, nervously.

'Easy, hoss,' Thwaites soothed it. 'Don't be scairt of ol' Pete now.'

A load was slung across the saddle like a couple of grain sacks, hanging either side. Thwaites edged forward, took the bridle and pulled the horse into the firelight. Its eyes were wild, its flanks lathered.

Thwaites saw these things were not entirely due to the exertion of the climb. The average cow pony did not relish the burden of a bloody corpse tied hands and feet to opposite stirrups.

'Waal, goddamn ... it's poor Arch Leggat, dead,' Thwaites breathed. 'Beaten so bad his face is nigh into a pulp.'

An eyeball was out of its socket and the head dangled at a grotesque angle, indicating Leggat's neck was broken.

'Brought up here a-purpose.'

Thwaites didn't have to tax his brain to work out what the purpose was: it was to warn him off; to tell him to quit before the same happened to him.

Bull Jusserand knew he was at the cave. He'd seen him off earlier with his Sharps. The beating Leggat had taken was just the kind Jusserand would take sadistic pleasure in meting out with his giant fists and hard boots. Leggat, tough and durable as whang-leather, would not have died quickly or easily.

Thwaites scratched his head, pondering. Jusserand's straight-line thinking could not readily be credited with the diabolic use

Leggat's grisly remains had been put to. The wordless warning, unsubtle though it was, bore the hallmarks of a cleverer yet no less cruel intellect.

It would be impossible to prove, but Thwaites guessed he was contemplating Franz Sturman's ruthless response to the irritating news that he was still in the district. Effectively, Jusserand was Sturman's blunt instrument.

But that didn't answer the bigger questions. Thwaites squatted by his dying fire, tin cup in gnarled hands, trying to stimulate his brain with black coffee. What had Leggat done to deserve death?

What had he come across that required his silence?

Kearny couldn't relax, even in Temperance's practised arms. He had to settle his mind about the scuffling sounds he'd heard through the hotel's walls. Temperance's glib speculations were not sufficient. More and more, he was niggled by doubts that she'd interpreted the disturbance rightly.

The next room was shared by Christine Smith and the well-fleshed girl called Sadie. Though he'd given begrudging credence to Temperance's report on the prior activities of Christine Smith, he still stuck to his gut feeling that she wasn't a seasoned whore and that she would have kept her word about retiring early to muster strength for the coach ride.

Eventually, Kearny could restrain himself no longer. He withdrew himself from the warmth of Temperance's greedy embrace. He left the bed, pulled on some clothes and put a spluttering sulphur match to the lamp.

'Where are you going?' Temperance asked, rousing herself.

'To check on – the other rooms.'

Temperance swung her legs off the bed, not trying to cover any of her lush nakedness. 'On Chrissie, you were going to say,' she said knowingly. 'Oh well, I'll come an' see you're not shocked by what she might've been up to.'

'Suit yourself, but put something on.'

'As if a lady wouldn't.'

In moments they were in the narrow upstairs passage between the third floor rooms.

'The door – it's been left open!' Alarm sharpened Kearny's low voice.

Temperance said, without much conviction, 'Maybe the girls wanted more air....'

But all her theories, her hoping, were

quickly dashed. They found the room un-occupied and in a shambles. The bed linen was strewn across the floor, and water had spilled from the porcelain jug tipped over on the washstand. The framed text in here was askew on the wall.

'I don't reckon they left willing,' Kearny said. 'There's all the signs of a struggle.'

Temperance let out her caught breath. 'Oh, God – they've been kidnapped! Where will we look for them?'

'Wherever men want women,' Kearny said, feeling sick. 'More exactly in this bailiwick, I'd say that means places where the customers aren't satisfied with the easy virtue of the local girls. Where they want white-skinned whores.'

'The saloons? The gambling dens? The dance halls?' Temperance despaired. 'Christ, where do we start?'

Kearny was collecting his shattered wits while cursing his earlier inaction. 'Let's light another lamp and start hunting clues right here,' he said. 'For a start, there's a peculiar smell.'

Temperance sniffed. 'It's chloroform,' she said as he lifted the lamp mantle.

'What's that?'

'It makes you drowsy, puts you to sleep.

It's used by midwives. A professor in Edinburgh started it, then Her Majesty Victoria had it when she whelped the eighth time. She called it soothing, quieting and delightful beyond all measure.'

Kearny was thoughtful. 'That means the girls' abductors came prepared. Maybe if they're put asleep they won't suffer.'

Temperance disabused him. 'I don't think they'll let them sleep long.'

The idea that Christine Smith was being ravished even as they spoke filled Kearny with near panic. Shadows were chased into the corners by the amber glow of the lit lamp. He shook his head irritably, as though to clear his thought processes. 'If only I didn't feel so damned used up!'

'Ain't no use for you to get mad at me,' Temperance said. 'Blame yourself.'

Kearny dropped his complaint, knowing it could lead only to time-wasting argument. He got on his knees and gathered up the ravelled bedsheet.

'Here! I've found something.'

Temperance shone the lamp on the item he'd placed on his open palm. It was a small precious stone spotted with red. 'It's a bloodstone, like from a ring,' she said.

Kearny said, 'It is from a ring. And I know

169

where I last saw it, or one very much like it. It was in a ring worn by the Irishman Finnegan!'

'That blasted whoreman! What can we do? Go to the governor?'

Kearny took the suggestion seriously. 'No. It'd take too long. Can't just us two together reform a boom town. I'll head for the construction camps pronto. That'll be best.'

Temperance shook her head. She looked less unconvinced than disgusted. 'You show up on Finnegan's stamping ground, asking questions, calling him out, they'll sure as hell kill you.'

Kearny's desperation lent him inspiration. 'I have an idea,' he said defiantly. 'I'll get myself into those camps before Finnegan knows it.'

Temperance still looked at him as though he was loco, but she said, 'All right – elaborate. Though first get this straight. I come, too. Someone will have to know where to put the flowers on your grave.'

13

FINNEGAN'S LAIR

Across town two hours later, but long before the sun would start lightening the eastern sky over the pine-clad peak of Sierra Mosca and the flat rooftops of the adobe houses, three spans of mules drew a 1,950 pound wagon and its 3,000 pounds of cargo out of a freighter's yard – a compound bare of a single blade of grass, set amidst a sprawl of ramshackle sheds and stables.

In compliance with city ordinances, the wagon moved at a sedate pace while inside town limits, to minimize churning up noisome dust from the hard-packed dirt and dried manure that formed the roadway out to the camps of the grading outfits.

Every day, heavy four-wheelers followed this route to haul out supplies for the ground-breaker crews preparing the way for the track layers of the newest stretch of rail-road. It was the freighting companies' last stand. Their dominant role in the West's system of transportation had been hugely reduced. Soon, they would provide little more than feeder services for the ubiquitous railroads.

The mules were sturdy, tough beasts, bred by putting Mexican jacks to well-proportioned draught mares. They were smart and astonishingly strong for their size. Leaving Santa Fe, their gait became a trot that jangled harness bells on their high collar bows and rattled trace chains.

The wagon driver, Trader Joe, was a wrinkled teamster with shoulders so hunched from long, laborious service in freighting that his head thrust forward on his baggy-skinned neck like a turtle's. A sealed, flat bottle of liquid gold from across the ocean had cost Will Kearny and Temperance more than her all-night fee, but it had made him very amenable to assisting them.

Temperance was dressed like a man in a worn shirt and trousers spared from Trader Joe's wardrobe. Though the garments were clean, they smelled faintly of booze. She travelled in the bed of the wagon, hunched down among bags and barrels. Kearny rode the seat alongside Joe.

They wheeled in an unreal, pre-dawn starlight over barren flats paralleling the new tracks till they came to a scattering of white tents and a row of clapboard buildings, new and half-erected. Fresh-painted signs identified most of these trackside structures as saloons and restaurants. On a siding were several dormitory cars, three decks high.

'Is Finnegan's place here?' asked Kearny.

'Naw, mister,' said Trader Joe, scratching his stubbled grey chin. 'This is end-of-tracks, where the engineers are. Finnegan is on ahead, among the grading layouts.'

Kearny studied on whether the rising town had a future, or whether it would simply have its day and become a weather-greyed ghost like many others that dotted the West. The rails were spreading fast; when Chinese labourers had been brought in to build the Central Pacific east from California, they had laid ten miles of track in a day to win a bet for ace construction superintendent Charles Crocker.

Kearny and Temperance got out of sight under a spread tarp. After Trader Joe had off-loaded sacks of flour and sugar and tobacco, he shook the reins and clucked up his team. Their path was now the roadbed prepared for the coming rails by dynamiters and pick and shovel workers who blasted and sliced across the landscape, rearranging rock that had been undisturbed for aeons.

The tent villages of the grading outfits, of which there appeared to be basically two, were more raw than the engineers' camp and showed no sign of permanence at all.

'Thar's Seamus Finnegan's, mister,' Joe said. He pointed a gloved finger toward a timbered ridge overlooking a line of sun-bleached slope stakes that had been placed by a survey team working beyond the camps. 'The railroad comp'ny keeps him at arm's length. Figger'tively speakin', he's a parasite, seein' the bosses don't hold with likker an' gamblin' an' wimmin. But they ain't much they kin do 'bout it. It's as nat'ral as a dog havin' fleas, an' the men gotta hev their fun someplace.'

Part-hidden behind the growth of piñon was a smaller group of tents.

Lights glimmered in the half-light up there despite the hour, and when Joe halted his clip-clopping team and the wheels of the wagon ceased grinding, Kearny heard the sounds of men's carousing carried down on the breeze.

'The boys are whoopin' it up late fer sure. Must of got somethin' to celebrate,' Joe said.

Temperance shivered. 'Maybe word's already about that Finnegan has brought in new attractions.'

Eyes blazing, teeth gritting, Kearny said, 'If the girls are there, I'll kill the bastard.'

Joe said gruffly, 'I ain't messin' in no *killin's,* mister. I got a livin' an' assets to consider. These mules o' mine are worth better'n hunn'erd dollars a head.'

'I'm not asking you to risk them. You drop us off at the foot of the ridge and go about your business. See that clump of trees?' Kearny pointed out an area of mesquite woodland in the deeply dark bottom of a wash between the construction camps and the ridge. 'You wait for us there after. Get us back to Santa Fe and there's another bottle in it for you.'

'What if yuh never show?'

Kearny shrugged. 'Then I guess we won't be around to get you into any hassles.'

The arrangement satisfied Trader Joe. He even managed to growl 'Good huntin'' when Kearny and Temperance jumped down from the wagon.

They struck up the steep grade toward the timber. Faint wind stirred the sparse growth of scraggly sage and brought a new sound to their ears, long and drawn out, keening above the raucous hoorawing of the drunken male revellers. It confirmed they were on no wild goose chase.

Temperance swore. 'That's Sadie – screaming something awful!'

Kearny felt the blood pound in his head, heating his face with its rush. In abducting the girls, Finnegan was not only seizing a source of revenue, he was also choosing a potently cruel and vicious way to repay his licking at the Lamy railroad station. Sadie was apparently still capable of objecting, but what had been done to Christine?

Kearny made a vow to himself that before dawn broke there was going to be a full settling-up.

'Finnegan'll pay for this with his life,' he raged.

'Unless they kill you first,' Temperance said.

Sadie's screaming was cut off suddenly amid slurred cursings. Kearny could imagine what had happened. One of her persecutors had struck her in the mouth to shut her up. They reached the timber line and forged into the black shadows of the piñons. Kearny thought he heard muffled sobbing, but it was quickly lost in the resumed hubbub of merriment.

The upward track Kearny chose switch-backed through the trees. It was little more than a game trail and let them approach under cover. They finished the ascent breathing hard.

Finnegan had established himself in a glade atop the ridge. He had a main tent some thirty by twenty feet. Behind it, several smaller shelters had been thrown up haphazardly and a short way off, a sturdy log cabin was in use. Kearny conjectured the cabin was the remnant of an earlier venture – maybe felling trees for use as lumber or firewood in Santa Fe.

Things were humming in the big tent. Light and lazy billows of tobacco smoke emanated from the open flap. A tough armed with a Greener was on lookout, lounging against a barrel. A hand-lettered sign on the barrel said: 'For admishun to show, throw in 2 silver dollars.'

Kearny said, low and harsh, 'Damn! Getting past him will alert the skunks inside.'

'No,' Temperance said. 'It doesn't have to. Listen....'

A minute later, the sentry looked up – and gawped in wonderment. A woman had come from nowhere and was casting about in the brush over by the edge of the trees.

He had no doubt it was a woman because she'd not bothered to button the shirt she wore, and it and what she had underneath swung loose and free as she leaned over as though choosing a spot.

He watched, engrossed, not thinking to call out, because a stranger woman up here could only be one of Finnegan's new whores and plainly represented no threat. Eventually, the woman seemed to find what she was looking for, lowered her trousers and squatted so he could see only the top of her head. The sentry giggled privately. The guys inside the tent weren't getting all the fun after all!

He heard a trickling stream splash dry leaves. Lust made his mouth water. Maybe he could wander on over and when she'd finished catch her unawares.

Tipping his hat at a rakish angle on his head, he put down the Greener and cat-footed to where she'd crouched out of sight in the cover of the brush.

'Gotcha with yuh pants down, girlie!' he rasped.

Then a second figure stepped out from behind a tree beside him. His hat was hurled off his head. Only a grunt of surprise escaped his lips before the barrel of a gun slammed hard against his skull, dropping him in a heap.

'Worked like a charm, didn't it?' Temperance said, pulling up her trousers. 'He can act out his fantasies in dreamland.'

Kearny handed Temperance the Colt in his fist. 'Keep out of the fracas if you can, but use this if I get in a tight. I'll collect the slumberer's shotgun.'

Pausing only to adjust his eyes to the lamplight around its opening, Kearny plunged into the tent, swinging the guard's Greener in a menacing arc.

'*Hoist your mitts!*' he snapped loudly. 'One false move and I'll cut the lot of you to bloody rags!'

No one argued with a shotgun, except maybe the blindest of drunks, and none of those present were quite that. Hands crept up above heads in the sudden hush.

The scene was totally ugly. Eight men were in the tent. One was a barkeeper with a yellow handlebar mustache. He stood twitching behind a bar built of raw pine lumber that ran almost across the far end. The others were railroad-labourer carousers, broad-shouldered and thick-bodied from swinging picks and mauls and shifting rock by shovel. They were in various stages of dress and inebriation.

One woman only was present. Black-eyed Sadie was stark naked on her back on a green-topped gaming table under which was dumped her torn night attire. Three of the burly customers had been holding her down in an enforced attitude of invitation with her legs lifted high.

'Easy, mister,' said one of the gang. 'There's enough woman here to last us all.' He dared to lower a hand to finger scratches on his cheek. 'She fought us like a wildcat, but them with meat on their bones can take slappin' about a bit afore they let yuh settle down to the business.'

Another bully-boy said, 'Why not git in line, mister? Thar's no need to be proddy; yuh'll git a piece. The filly's up to plenty more humpin' even if she ain't tight no more.'

Sadie moaned unintelligibly. Her head rolled from side to side. She was in a pitiful state. Her round face was puffed up and her eyes were slits amid the bruising. Her lips were puffed, split and bleeding; her body blotched with bruises.

'Get away from her,' Kearny said, spitting out his contempt. 'There's men and there's men.'

'They's women an' women,' returned a labourer too drunk to recognize an insult but imbued with the smart-mouthed wisdom of the bottle.

'Where's the other girl?' Kearny asked. He jerked the formidable Greener, hypnotizing them with the gaping twin barrels. They needn't have broken Sadie's face; that they had made him fear they'd already ruined Christine irretrievably and disposed of her.

The barkeep shuffled like a nervous horse. 'The ittybitty 'un? She'll be over to Finnegan's – the big cabin.'

'What've they done to her?'

'Nothin'. Finnegan said this 'un was no Rose of Tralee an' to put her to work directly, seein' the boys ain't seen a new white woman in weeks. But he figgered to keep the skinny mophead back for startin' by auction. Said she'd be a goldmine. Me, I reck'n he fancied doin' some sample minin' hisself.'

Kearny's anxiety was unrelieved. With a lift of the shotgun he pointed out one of two hanging oil lamps, circled by moths, that illuminated the brutal scene. 'Get a chair, barkeep, snuff out that lamp and bring it down.'

The barkeeper carried out the order. His fingers fumbled and his legs almost buckled as he came down off the chair.

Kearny nodded approvingly. 'Now tip out the oil, up the back of the tent and around the bar, you miserable runt. Do it, damn you – fast!'

The trembling barkeeper splashed the oil around as directed until the lamp was empty. 'Is that all?' he asked.

'No,' Kearny said curtly. 'The girl's out of it.' Sadie seemed totally unaware of what was going on; when she opened her blackened eyelids, her eyes were vacant and unseeing. 'Carry her over here with her clothes and put her at my feet. And no tricks, mind, any of you. My trigger finger's purely tensed-up.'

Sadie, exhausted and in shock, was a listless, shivering weight in the barkeeper's arms, but he dragged her over.

'Get back with the others,' Kearny snapped at him. He crooked the shotgun in his right arm and pulled out matches from his pocket.

Left-handed, he eased a lucifer from the box and wiped its head across the rough denim over his thigh. Then he tossed it burning toward the bar.

Whoosh!

The oil ignited with a flash, jumped the bar and roared up the canvas back of the tent. The startled patrons were now caught between two fires, one of them literal.

'Stop that if you can,' Kearny told them. 'But don't anyone try stopping me. I've got help outside, and I've still got the Greener.'

He flung the horribly docile Sadie over his shoulder, covering her sticky body as best he could with her tattered garment, and took out.

Temperance was waiting for him in the blackness of the trees. She'd been wisely busy. The tent's doorman had regained consciousness, but she'd already trussed him wrists to ankles with his belt and stuffed his dirty kerchief in his mouth. As a felicitous touch, she'd pulled down the lobo's beltless pants, baring his buttocks and privates as recompense in kind for her self-humiliation in the cause of his removal.

She took in Sadie's battered countenance and blank state of mind. 'Jesus, what have they done to her?' she said.

'The usual, but rougher and overmuch of it. Help her down to the mesquite grove. I'm going for Christine.'

With these perfunctory words, Kearny raced off. The tent was burning fiercely. He skirted the red, smoky glare – where silhouetted figures battled frantically to stop the fire's spread – and headed for the old log cabin.

He reached it as the door lurched open on creaking hinges, creating a pallid pool of lampglow on the porch. Seamus Finnegan, dressed in a grey woollen undervest and longjohns staggered out, blinking in wild amazement at the blaze and the towering plume of smoke.

'Sweet Mary, me saloon is taken on fire! Stop it, ye damn fools!' he bellowed at the firefighters. But their own shouts and the crackle of flames made them oblivious to him.

From the cabin behind him, came a girl's cry. 'Help me, someone! Help!' Kearny recognized Christine's voice, desperate and tinged with hopelessness. Left by herself, she was pluckily seizing what was possibly a first and momentary chance to call out.

Finnegan snarled over his shoulder, 'Shut up, ye little slut, or ye'll go to all-comers, like your blowzy sister!'

Kearny saw red that had nothing to do with the blaze he'd started. He charged forward, tasting the scents of pine and burning on his deep breaths. He swung up the Greener and cold-bloodedly squeezed the trigger.

The stock of the ten-gauge shotgun

bucked against his shoulder and deafened him with its thunderclap. An instant's orange flash was swallowed in coiling black smoke.

Finnegan was slammed back against the wall of his cabin by the force of the blast. Tinkling glass fell from a window that caught and was shattered by the edge of the devastating buckshot pattern. A mess of red blotted the grubby wool stretched over Finnegan's gross gut. He looked down at the shredded fibres and pumping blood, his incredulity blackly comic.

'Ye've kilt me, bejasus!' he wheezed with his agonized last breaths. He was nigh cut in two. He clutched his belly, guts spilling through his pudgy fingers, and sat down in the dirt and drifted pine needles. Then he toppled over, a gory ruin.

Kearny said to no one, 'A quick death. You deserved slower, louse.'

Feeling no remorse, only a sick dismay about the plight in which he might find Christine, he plunged into the cabin.

It had one oblong room fitted out with a rough-made deal table and chairs, a blackened potbelly stove and a bed. His stomach turned. The place stank of smoke, the rancid grease drippings of old meals and a musky trace of copulation.

Christine was lashed by her wrists to the bed. She still wore her nightgown, but it was bunched around her shoulders. To Kearny's relief her delicate-featured face was undamaged and didn't have the haunting emptiness he'd seen in Black-eyed Sadie's.

But he was wrenched by how she tried to coil up her thin body in a pathetic bid to hide the places where abuse marked her fine, smooth skin. She turned her face into a brown-stained pillow.

'Dear Lord, I'm so glad to see you. I knew you'd search for us, even if everyone else thought nothing of it. Then, when I heard the shooting....' She let her shaky words hang.

'Finnegan got his needings. Sent to a place where I don't think he'll meet Saint Pat.'

'Death ... it dogs my descent,' she said. 'And more shame! A gentleman must be shocked to find me like this.'

Kearny was already cutting her loose with his boot knife. He said hoarsely, 'No call to blame yourself. Finnegan plainly took you by force, and he's paid for it in spades. His stinking soul burns in hell. Are you – hurt?'

She pulled down her gown and rubbed her wrists. She shuddered and her eyes avoided his. 'Not really. It was nothing not done to me before,' she said. 'A bath would make a world of difference.'

Now was not the time for Kearny to ponder the vexing paradox of a girl who could regret shame but was prepared to wing her way West as a soiled dove. A bath he couldn't offer.

He rolled up the moth-sampled red blankets from the bed. He also took down a duster hanging from a nail. 'Put this around you. We have to duck away from here fast. Here, I can't expect you to make it on your own two feet. I'll give you a lift over my shoulder.'

'Thank you – but no,' she said. 'I think I'm equal to a little running. Carrying me would slow you down.'

'You're a good soldier,' he said.

In the spreading light of sun-up, they snuck through the long shadows of the pine belt and hurried down to the mesquite woodland. Trader Joe, Temperance and Sadie awaited them.

'I was worried,' Temperance said. 'Particularly when the goose gun blasted. You're sure no one's tagging you?'

Kearny shook his head. 'Seems like every mother's son's busy stopping the spread of the fire.'

Trader Joe put his mules into brisk motion and Christine and Sadie, rolled in the frayed red blankets, fell into exhausted sleep.

14

A SHOOTING ON MAIN STREET

The unscheduled, privately chartered stage-coach bringing Rawhide Fork's six prospective brides was two days out from Santa Fe and had another two to reach its destination.

The journey was being taken in shortish legs, spelling the horses at regular intervals. Will Kearny rode his reliable chestnut up the dusty road apiece from the 'tumbleweed' coach.

Though bone tired, he'd been better than willing to depart the territorial capital shortly after returning there with Trader Joe and the three women. Seamus Finnegan's operations had been of doubtful legitimacy and he'd not anticipated the tent saloon-man's erstwhile associates making his demise a law-and-order issue, but he'd no wish to be entangled in a chance hue and cry.

Sadie had been seen by a doctor at

Temperance's insistence and expense. The medico had huffed and puffed but cleared her to travel. Her physical injuries weren't grave. Reassuringly, after being violently sick, she'd emerged from the shell into which she'd withdrawn, expressing anger to her companions about the bruising vicious-ness of her gang-rape.

Christine had reassumed her odd serenity. But Kearny believed her straight-glancing, violet-blue eyes were tinged with a faint regret. He found himself inhibited from approaching her. He couldn't make out whether that was a result of having seen her unclothed and recently used, or something else.

The stage road followed a twisting river. Irrigated fields growing green patches of grain were scattered with Mexican villages at intervals along its banks. If Kearny hadn't been slouched in the saddle, wearied and with a sense of desolation, he might have seen before the coach driver a banner of dust over the road ahead.

'A rider coming up,' called the alert whip.

The approaching horseman saw the coach and boosted his mount into a lope that quickly ate up the distance between them. Long before he was bearing down, Kearny recognized both man and horse. 'Doggone it, Pete Thwaites and his Kentucky black.'

Thwaites slackened the pace as he drew near, came on at a wary trot and reined up. 'If'n it ain't Will Kearny,' he greeted his ex-foreman. 'I heered yuh was ridden to Santa Fe fer them crooks, Sturman an' his lawyer tool Reece. What goes on here?'

Kearny gave a terse resume of their misadventures. Thwaites listened silently. But all the while his boggling eyes surveyed the bevy of onlooking women. Suddenly he said, 'Hell's bells! They ain't nothin' but go-around drawer-droppers, Will. A body can near smell 'em. Yuh playin' along with Sturman's schemes, huh?'

Temperance said feistily, 'Are you talking about us, old man? You may be a friend of Mr Kearny's, but it don't give you a right to insult us. Why, there's more dirt in your mind than in an unswamped stable. Drawer-droppers, my ass! Your eyes have been fair stripping the clothes off us since you got here.'

'Weren't talkin' nohow to you, woman. Hush your mouth!'

Kearny moved round, putting his wide shoulders between them. He tugged at Thwaites's sleeve. 'Leave it, the pair of you,' he said, drawing Thwaites aside. 'Tell me, Pete, what's been happening around Rawhide Fork and where are you riding?'

'The valley's gone from bad to worse.' Pete shook with angry emotion. 'Murder's bin done. They got Arch Leggat. His spur has rung its knell.'

Kearny stiffened, the shock of his old partner's untimely death knifing through him. This was worse news than he'd expected. 'How did it happen, and why?' he asked harshly.

Thwaites told what little he knew; his suspicion that Leggat had been in a fight with Arrowhead's Bull Jusserand.

'The town's gotten rougher an' more lawless by the day. Respectable folks are quittin'. Sturman's recruited extra scum – the border-jumper type, more gunslicks than cowhands, fellers on the dodge... If I was to stay thereabouts, I'd get sick o' watchin' the grief gatherin' up.'

Kearny frowned. 'What's in it for them, Pete?'

'Damned if I know – yet. Thought you might, seein' how it looks like yuh've gone over to the winnin' side.'

'I'd no choice, Pete,' Kearny said, put out by his old boss's blunt speaking. 'It wasn't done as treachery to old friends.'

Thwaites's criticism was especially hard to take, since it was the cantankerous ranch owner's prior quitting of the Rocking T that had left him high and dry.

Thwaites jerked his calloused thumb, indicating the six women behind him.

'It sure ain't gonna help Rawhide Fork none shippin' in a cargo o' trollops.'

They were supposed to be gentlefolk, enlisted by the town council to soothe savage breasts and make good wives,' Kearny said with an attempt at irony.

'Then y'all bin bamboozled some,' Thwaites declared. 'That's a sorry troupe, ev'ry one of 'em.'

'I disagree,' Kearny said with quiet firmness. 'They're not all cut out of the same bolt of cloth. At least one isn't beyond redemption.'

Thwaites deigned to turn and give a second look, but his stare was offensively knowing. 'The skinny one with the frizzed-out hair? Naw, she's got a past, mark my words.'

Thwaites's hostile opinion goaded Kearny. 'Some secrets maybe,' he conceded stiffly. 'More sinned against than sinning.'

Thwaites laughed sardonically. 'Sweet on

her, are yuh? Tread careful, less'n she two-times yuh. Thar's not a thing yuh can do about it, Will. Money buys any o' them women. They all got their price. That un'll turn out no diff'rent from the rest in the passel, though I allow she ain't toil-worn – she's purty.'

Kearny's mouth tightened. 'I wasn't looking for your good opinion,' he said, regretting having let his feelings show almost before he knew them himself.

Thwaites shrugged. 'Gotta take m'self to Santa Fe. I'll be gettin' along. Why don't yuh dump this bad lot an' kick in with me? She'll be hell-roarin' in Rawhide Fork.'

'No, Pete. I'm sticking it out. The town's trusted me with its money and I've got to deliver.'

'Then I pity yuh fer a sucker, Will. Jest make sure they don't blame yuh fer what it is yuh delivers. That's all I gotta say.'

Pete Thwaites jogged off, leaving Kearny wondering what was waiting for him in Rawhide Fork. The news had been grim, disturbing. Vermin drifting in; his friend Arch Leggat murdered. God, there was an evil day's work!

It sounded a tinderbox situation. Which was why he had to press on.

Abandoned to fate in such an environment and at such a wrong time, a girl like Christine Smith might easily come to grief where a man would make his way somehow.

Kearny had been away from Rawhide Fork shy of two weeks, but he thought he could see the ominous signs of change the minute he rode into the town's dusty main stem.

The previously paintless and weathered grey siding of the First Claim had been coated a garish yellow. A sign daubed in red declared the premises to be the Pleasure Palace. Kearny remembered the pails of paint he'd seen stashed in the back room of Seth Mallison's saloon. So this was the use to which they'd been put. He shook his head wonderingly.

Black-eyed Sadie tugged back a leather window curtain and looked out from the tumbleweed Concord. She took in the amateurish paint job on the saloon and the straggle of otherwise unpretentious buildings petering out at the nearest end to empty lots where sun-browned scrub was littered with old cans and empty bottles.

'Jesus, what a hole! It looks like the back of nowhere.'

An Arrowhead party was on a visit to town.

Franz Sturman's men were hanging around in aimless clusters under the awnings, in the sparse tree shade and along the plankwalks. Some of the faces were new to Kearny, but he recognized them all as belonging to the outlaw breed Pete Thwaites had described. The men's indefinable, restless air of anticipation was also familiar to him. It told him trouble was a-building.

What were they were waiting for?

It didn't immediately occur to him – as it should – that word travels fast across the prairies, whisked as intangibly but surely ahead like the message of an Indian smoke signal, and that the idling groups awaited the imminent arrival of the stage.

The biggest crowd of roughnecks included Bull Jusserand and was around the stage company's yard, where the hired coach driver brought the jangling trot of his team to a halt. The company's town agent scuttled out from the office and said the driver was to let his passengers alight and put his rig in the yard.

It impinged on Kearny's sharpened consciousness that the area was also largely absent of other townsfolk, almost as though they'd retreated, abandoning the street to the Arrowhead crew.

The coach disgorged the women. The watching loafers raised a ragged cheer. Kearny glowered and the tumult degenerated into whistles and catcalls. Some of the men were plainly liquored up.

'Ignore them,' Kearny said. 'They're fool drunk and full of funny ideas.'

A girl with hennaed hair said, 'They've got ideas all right, but I don't know that a travel-sick gal would find 'em funny.'

'Howsoever,' added Temperance, forever practical, 'business is where it pops up an' tomorrow will be another day.'

The stage company's man and the driver were busy organizing the unloading of the women's bags. A platform at the rear of the coach was held by straps strung from the corners of the roof and was enclosed in black oiled leather to form a weatherproof boot.

The agent said to Kearny, 'The bags've got to go to the hotel, an' the passengers put up there. Mr Reece's say-so.'

Kearny looked around, frowning. 'Where is Seabury Reece?'

The agent shrugged. 'Couldn't say. He said he wasn't directly involved and you were taking care of things.'

This bothered Kearny some more, but he

was given no chance to pursue it.

Bull Jusserand had ambled over to the group back of the coach. He hoisted Temperance's carpetbag in a big mitt like it was a pocket-size sack of tobacco, stuffed it under his arm and picked up a second. 'Carry the bags, ma'am.' His tongue, coarse always, slobbered over the words and the dark balls of his eyes, fixing not on Temperance's face but her full bosom, were bright with lust.

'Aw, move aside, Bull, yuh homely numbskull. Yuh'll crush the ladies' delicate stuff, way you go 'bout a chore.'

The speaker was another of the hardcase Arrowhead company – one of the newcomers Kearny hadn't seen before, full of booze, and careless or ignorant of the nature of the man he was speaking to. He also winked at Temperance, who tittered.

Jusserand had a brute's hatred of being laughed at – especially by women whom he sensed were repulsed by his extreme ugliness. He dropped the bags he'd picked up around his feet and hit the new Arrowhead rider across the mouth.

'I don't like your gab, Dysart!'

For Jusserand, it was fly-swat stuff – just delivering mild reproof.

But the man Dysart wasn't taking it

198

lightly. Nor was Dysart so drunk that he didn't know Jusserand would squash him if he took him on hand to hand. Sent reeling back, he grabbed for his gun. He was striving to recover balance on his tottering, high-heeled boots. He was snarling, telegraphing his intention.

Kearny saw the danger instantly. With the women and the stage-company men all around Jusserand, Dysart was likely to injure or kill an innocent party. With Dysart's weapon clearing leather, Kearny himself drew and fired.

He didn't have time to aim and didn't see where he hit Dysart, but the gunhawk stood gazing stupidly at the gun he was pointing at the group, then he slowly folded and fell on his face, his gun exploding harmlessly.

The stage driver gawped at Kearny. 'Never see'd yuh draw it, mister. It was jest in your hand. Quickest shootin' I ever saw!'

'Mr Kearny sure handled his iron faster than the Arrowhead gunnie,' said the company agent.

Kearny felt no satisfaction, only huge regret over the sudden and startling affray. He'd not shot to kill Dysart, but he knew he was dead.

'You'd think he'd have better sense than to shoot down one of your top – uh – cowhands, Mr Sturman. Such men don't come cheap.'

Seabury Reece, all apology, was delivering his urgent report of the past hour's happenings in Rawhide Fork to Franz Sturman in his sponsor's front parlour at Arrowhead headquarters. The lawyer felt intimidated by the trappings of solid wealth around him – the massive pieces of fine oak furniture, the seldom-used but good piano, a huge and original Spanish oil painting of bathing nymphs in an ornate gilt frame.

'Why don't you say it, Seabury?' said Sturman drily, tapping ash from his stogie. 'One of my professional gunfighters, paid a hundred a month, has been wiped out by a has-been range boss.'

Reece gulped. 'And afterward, I hear tell, a woman with bleached ringlets gave Kearny a passionate kiss right on the street – as if he were a very Byron. It discomfited him mightily and was an affront to public decency.'

'Jim dandy!' Sturman beamed. 'Couldn't be better. He brings in these whores, provokes a ruckus with 'em right off, brashly goes to shooting, bills and coos in plain sight... Yeah, it won't be hard to lay all the

200

blame on his shoulders. Our smart-alecky catspaw will get his claws drawn. He'll be finished. So will Rawhide Fork, almost directly. Meanwhile, our hands are purely clean of the messy business. What more can we ask?'

Sturman's encouraging comments and the warmth of a generous swallow of his expensive whiskey did much to settle the trepidation that had been fluttering in Reece's stomach.

When Will Kearny found Reece's door solidly shut and locked against him, the lawyer absent from his practice, he felt the beginnings of a crisis of morale. He'd been out of his depth through essential parts of the mission to Santa Fe. Now he wanted badly to collect the money still coming and cast off. The shooting to unintended death of an obvious curly wolf in what was the closest he had to a home town had been the last straw.

Yet he also knew deep down it wasn't merely an easy matter of seeing Reece, picking up the *dinero* and handing over his responsibilities for six women's shelter and feeding.

Temperance Doe, Black-eyed Sadie and

the rest would maybe know how to deal with whatever it was the revamped Rawhide Fork had in mind for them, but try as he might his thoughts kept returning to the conscience-pricking subject of Christine Smith.

Despite everything that had been done to her, she kept a prim honesty in her open face. When she was scrubbed clean of unnecessary artifice and the freshness was on her like dew, she was the young innocent you'd expect to meet going into church on a Sunday. He wanted to be her protector, but he didn't know how to do that because he knew he was unworthy and that his approach might easily be construed as self-serving and interfering.

For that matter, his understanding of the young woman was also woefully in-adequate. What would he be interfering with? Why was she so sure it was Rawhide Fork where she wanted to be? She'd steadfastly avoided revealing this to anyone. All women were complicated – even plain-speaking ones like Temperance – but Christine Smith struck Kearny as being the most baffling of all.

Pete Thwaites's verdict had been uncom-promising. Without her pretty face, he'd have sense enough to know her for what she was.

After leaving Reece's, Kearny decided against returning immediately to the hotel, where he'd left the women resting. He cut across to the First Claim Saloon – or, as it now proclaimed itself, the Pleasure Palace. Idlers parted respectfully to let him through the batwing doors.

The exterior renovations were nothing compared to the transformation within. The First Claim had been a sawdust dump; the Pleasure Palace was something else. Though it was too early for the rush of evening-trade, the place was humming. Games of chance other than poker had been introduced. A roulette wheel whirred. Faro and dice were in progress to the chants of sleeve-less dealers and dicemen who were strangers to Kearny but had the frozen-faced look of professionals.

Carpet had been laid on the stairs to the gallery, suggestive of luxurious accommodations in the private rooms to which they gave access. The several large paintings that decorated the walls were of nudes – typically, a voluptuous wench inexplicably lolling in her birthday suit on a velvet, drawing-room couch in a pose that showed most of everything.

The old counter had been stripped out and replaced with an elegant rosewood bar. A ceiling-high backbar mirror seemed to double the size of the room, reflecting all the polished brass and cut-glass fittings, including a huge chandelier.

Seth Mallison and his rotund barkeeper still worked behind the bar, but they wore scarlet sateen shirts with white ties.

Kearny wended his way through the nondescript throng of customers to give an order for a pitcher of beer to Mallison.

The sallow-faced saloon keeper smirked as 'he pulled the pump's carved wood handle. 'We've been working hard since you've been gone, Kearny. How do you like the changes?'

Kearny affected nonchalance. 'It ain't the fanciest drinking spot I ever did see, though it shoots close. I guess the house takes a commission on the gaming play, but only one man around here has the wherewithal to bankroll such a set-up. What is Franz Sturman getting out of it?'

Mallison's grin became sleety. 'I don't discuss business arrangements and I'm not privy to Mr Sturman's intentions. Maybe you should ask his attorney, Mr Reece, though I doubt you could give him good reason to tell you.'

He pushed across Kearny's beer and turned to a cowpoke bellying up to another part of the bar.

Kearny ignored the rudeness and took himself to an empty table in the quietest corner. But even here the click and rattle of dice and chips was inescapable. He noted the absence of the town's more sober-sided citizens and the proliferation of transient types, gunslung and steel-eyed. An establishment like this in a place with no law officer would be a magnet for scum and troublemakers. He wondered if the games were rigged – the dice loaded and the roulette wheel specially geared.

Hell ... it wouldn't take much of a spark to cause an explosion that would blow the town wide open.

Looking around at the incipient corruption and the tawdry glitter, Kearny found one thing missing in the Pleasure Palace. Where were the house-girls with short skirts and painted faces, working the room to charm the suckers into parting with their money? And negotiating hour-long retirements into privacy that hinged on the purchase of over-priced bottles of champagne?

His beer backed up in his throat and he near choked.

God, what a fool he'd been! The required women were right on hand, freshly delivered by himself! The leading citizens had been duped into providing hurdy girls free of cost and comebacks through the hopeful 'brides' scheme.

At the Stardust Hotel some hours later, Temperance came right out and let Kearny know she was available to warm his bed, anywhere, anytime – business allowing, of course – till further notice.

Though she was bidding fair to chase after him like a bitch in heat, Kearny had developed a peculiar respect for Temperance. Undeniably, also, he would enjoy obliging her. But the days he'd spent on horseback reaching Santa Fe, his hectic time in and around the capital, the return ride and latterly a sorrows-drowning bout of drinking, had left him drained of energy. He declined the immediate invitation and settled for the comforts of a bed unshared.

Mulling over the unfortunate killing of the gunslinger Dysart and his other problems, he lapsed into an exhausted sleep.

The clustered frame and adobe buildings that made up Rawhide Fork were baking in the forenoon sun when he set out on a

second attempt to make contact with Seabury Reece.

He didn't make it past the front of the
general store operated by Ramon Martinez,
the mayor of Rawhide Fork. Martinez, a
small, brisk man in his early forties, called
him in, promptly closed his doors and took
off his apron.

Kearny had a notion removal of the apron
was meant to signify a casting-off of Martinez' storekeeper role and the assumption
of mayoral duty. If so, the gesture was futile.
Mingled store aromas, dominated by coffee
beans and coal oil, pervaded the dim,
goods-stacked interior.

'Will Kearny, the town council is disgusted
with your doings,' Martinez declaimed indignantly. 'Your action in shooting a man to
death in plain view on Main Street yesterday
was ill-timed, hasty, offensive and downright
illegal.'

Kearny was taken aback by the storekeeper's tone, by the unhedged censure in
his words, but he was quick to defend himself. 'It wasn't intentional: I shot only
because I had to. The man was a gunslinger
and he went for his iron first. Bystanders
were apt to get hurt, maybe killed. Though
it wasn't my argument, I'd no choice.

Haven't you been told that?'

'I know that the argument was provoked by a woman – one of those creatures brung here by yourself, Kearny,' Martinez said.

'Beg pardon, Mr Martinez. I didn't promote the idea to import the women. According to Mr Reece, it was rightfully the decision of the council and the mayor – namely yourself.'

'Pshaw! You misrepresent my meaning.' Distaste pinched Martinez' harsh features. 'Where was your own good sense, man? The females are plainly not the clean-living, deserving women a law-abiding community expected.'

Kearny was put on the back foot, confronted with the obvious. 'I didn't hire on to pass judgement,' he said flatly.

'They're troublemaking harlots, every one. Fine, decent men built this town and I'm damned if I'll stand by and let them make it over into a bawdy strip. A fight and a man shot within minutes of their coming – why, it speaks for itself! They should be tarred and feathered and driven out of town, with whips if that's what it takes.'

Kearny could see himself being set up as a scapegoat for the gathering problems.

'Sure, Rawhide Fork was formerly a quiet

community without many brawls, but I seem to recollect it was you and your council who were persuaded to let Marshal Gurney go,' he accused. 'Maybe the truth of it is that you and the towners have been deceived by Franz Sturman and his lawyer.'

'I don't believe it,' Martinez said, excessively adamant. 'Show me your evidence before you start throwing mud at your betters, Kearny. Sturman is a powerful man. Why should he want to wreck this town? You're deliberately straying from the point, which is you've let our money be misspent on sinful women fit only for a whorehouse and for sparking fights and gunplay.'

'This parley is getting boresome, Mr Mayor,' Kearny said. 'If it's the same to you, I ain't staying to have my ears chawed off.'

Kearny unlatched the doors himself and pushed out. He went from the mercantile to Seabury Reece's place and again found it locked up and deserted.

Reece was the only man in town Kearny could think of who might be prevailed on to clarify his position. Frustrated, the noon heat beating down, he retraced his tracks to the hotel. His boots raised dust clouds that spread out and hung in a still stratum marking his path.

15

ROADS TO RUIN

Only Christine Smith showed unease when Temperance Doe told her and the other girls of the proposition that had been put up by the proprietor of the Pleasure Palace saloon.

Sadie and the others accepted it stoically. They'd way back abandoned hope of any other sort of life. You hawked your body, you subsisted. Society accepted, if not acknowledged, that this was the ineradicable, natural order of things.

'I'd hoped to leave that behind me, in New York City,' Christine said in a small voice.

Temperance scoffed. 'Don't feed us that line, dearie. The fairy-tale in the newspaper notices was just for appearances. You were warned, but wanted along anyhow.'

Christine sighed. 'Working in a saloon really wasn't what I came here for.'

'God, she not only looks like a madonna,' said the girl with the hennaed hair, 'she's starting to act like one.'

'Well, it's a bit late for playing the Virgin Mary now,' Temperance said.

Christine had no wish to alienate the troupe of whores. She'd thrown in her lot with them and permitted herself to be led. Despite their low regard for morality as taught by her mama – who, if alive and possessing an inkling of her escapades, would have long since been scandalized – the women had by any lights been good to her. By and large, they'd treated her fairly. Shelter and friendship now had to be repaid. She'd no excuse for wriggling out.

A little later, with her cheeks still tinged by their coarse ribbing, Christine accompanied the party when it shifted, bags and baggage, to the hideous yellow building that was the saloon.

Above its upper windows, blazoned in crude red letters on the falsefront, was the legend Pleasure Palace. She also saw it repeated over the main door with smaller lettering underneath: *Seth Mallison, Prop.*

Temperance looked at her strangely. 'What's the matter, Chrissie? You look like you're about to cry. It won't be so bad. Our rooms are newly done out an' clean as a new pin. A girl could get a lot worse. I thought we'd gotten rid of that second thoughts nonsense. You aren't planning on running out on us, are you?'

Christine shuddered lightly. 'Oh, no. I won't do that. In fact, I'm sure *now* this is just where I want to stay.'

It was exactly what Temperance wanted to hear and she didn't question her change of heart. But not long after, when Christine voiced the same desire to stay to Will Kearny – put on their trail by the Stardust Hotel lobby clerk – it was another matter.

He looked at her, lips tightened as though to bottle up the anger that made his chest heave. At last he said, 'Hell! I'd had a better opinion of you, Miss Smith. How did you get mixed up in this mess?'

'What do you mean?' she asked, her knees oddly trembling. They were in her new room. He'd come in not announcing himself other than with a commanding knock, and she was embarrassed.

The room was furnished with a low, wide cot and a three-mirrored dresser on which stood a porcelain basin and pitcher. Behind a sleazy black satin curtain on a rail were a shiny copper bathtub and a stack of towels which someone had sprinkled with a cheap, cloying perfume that had spread everywhere.

Worse, she'd also been trying out a cos-tume supplied for the reception of visitors other than Will Kearny: a flimsy cambric shift cut so that loose shoulder straps con-stantly slipped to give peeps of the darker pink that haloed her nipples.

'Mallison is part of the plot to ruin this town,' Kearny began through gritted teeth. 'His premises have been made over for crooked gambling and prostitution. There'll be fights, gunplay and back-alley stabbings, sure as night follows day. You can see this is a bawdy house – yet you want to work here. That means you've chosen to be something I'd dared to hope you weren't.'

Christine felt the reproach like a lash. And a voice inside her head – her mother's? – whispered that he was right and all this was wrong. But her spirit insisted she answered back.

'Maybe you presume, Mr Kearny. With all that's happened to me, why should I expect to do any different from Temperance and the others? Perhaps I was made for it – naturally predisposed. Moreover, my choices and arrangements are none of your concern.'

He groaned. 'Yeah, that's true as far as it goes. And I can't say as I blame you. Nor do I want to preach at you. But this is no way to find a better life. Offering yourself to men for money is making yourself cheap. I'm deeply sorry for you, Miss Smith.'

'You don't have to be,' she said, turning her back on him so she didn't have to meet his accusing gaze, or let him see the tears pricking her eyes. 'I think it would be best if you left and didn't try to see me again!'

She forced the words out in a snap, knowing they hurt herself as much they could him. It was suddenly very clear and very saddening. He'd come out of his way to lecture her – no easy thing for a man of his kind. He wouldn't be admonishing her unless he felt something else that he wasn't saying.

And it didn't finish there. She wouldn't be feeling so bad over the loss of his good opinion either, unless she, too, felt the same thing. She'd known it days since, but had dismissed it, knowing it would do no good for it to come out in the open. She was in love with him; he with her.

'Go! Go! Go!' she blurted in an undamable excess of emotion.

There came a loud knocking on the door. 'Miss Smith!' a man's voice called. 'Miss Smith, you all right?'

Kearny called back, 'Don't you fret yourself none about the young lady, Mallison. She's fine – so far.'

Mallison repeated, 'Miss Smith? I thought I heard you raise your voice. Who's in there?'

Christine had no idea what to say. 'It was – er – a mistake. The gentleman is a visitor about to leave.'

'Satisfied?' Kearny asked.

'Nope,' said Mallison. 'Men ain't being entertained in these rooms without due payment. I recognize your voice, Will Kearny, and I'm a-coming in. From now on, you got no more prior rights than any other feller in Rawhide Fork.'

The doorknob twisted and the unbolted door opened. 'Out, Kearny!' Mallison ordered. 'The girls' time's gotta be paid for. No stud gets to sneak up my stairs.'

To Christine, the tension was palpable. Kearny stared at the saloon keeper with repugnance, as though he was an obscene worm crawled out from a cesspit. Christine had no stomach for the explosion she sensed coming.

Kearny spat out his words. 'You're a stinking, weak-kneed bastard, Mallison, worse than I ever suspected. You've let the First Claim be turned into a den of vice. I

216

despise you and your damned belief a man's call is just to stay alive and make money.'

Mallison came no closer than the doorframe, but his sallow face darkened with a vicious hate. 'Kearny, you try bucking Sturman and Reece and you'll be riding for a big fall. You ain't bothering the girls no more and they'd damn well better believe it. They're under my orders now.'

Christine's heart quailed when Kearny gestured toward her.

'Maybe this one won't dance to your tune if she gets smart to your dragging her down,' he said, his voice filled with scorn. 'She's had a bad run of luck, but if her pride and pluck hold out, she's still got a chance to change it.'

Mallison sneered. 'So that's it, Kearny. You're soft on her, huh? Well, it makes no difference. You pay same as anyone. She's green-broke enough to know what she's in for: more boys through her bed than a cat gets fleas.' He laughed. 'Hell! Could be while she's still narrow-hipped and tight I'll treat me to finding out how she is myself.'

Alarm sent Christine's pulses racing. 'Oh no!' she cried. 'You must never do that. You really mustn't.'

Too late, she saw that Mallison's suggestion and her horrified cry at its unwitting vileness had turned Will Kearny's heavy contempt for the saloon man into an over-boiling agony. The blood mounted to his face; his eyes clouded stormily. He bunched his fists and raged, 'That's dirty talk, Mallison. Put 'em up!'

He was dancing forward and Mallison's fists came up defensively. Aghast at what she'd precipitated, Christine watched Kearny's first jab take Mallison full on the nose. She didn't think it was a dangerous blow, but it was a painful one, bringing tears flooding Mallison's eyes and an almost immediate stream of red from the target.

Mallison loosed a cuss-word and hit back, a right cross that Kearny received on the jaw. Christine wanted to look away but couldn't. In awful fascination, she witnessed a rapid exchange of punches, mostly to the face and head.

Kearny's anger was so fierce he hardly seemed to notice any damage Mallison inflicted on him. He soaked up with no more than sparse grunts the punishment of a series of swings and uppercuts that created livid swells and lumps.

Again and again, Christine couldn't stop from flinching at the smacking impacts of the barefisted blows. The ugly fight gave her no satisfaction at all.

Mallison was probably ten years Kearny's senior. Another disadvantage was that he was not in the fighting trim that years of hard range work had produced in the younger man. Kearny was also three inches taller and had a longer reach.

The outcome was inevitable.

Mallison clipped Kearny under the chin with a right hook that left him exposed to Kearny's fast left. The slamming blow caught Mallison on the side of the head, rocking him back on his heels to a standstill, staring glassily. He took a deep, gulping breath, clutching at his chest, swaying like an axed tree in the split-second before it topples. Then all intelligence left his slack features and he crashed headlong to the floor.

An instinctive awareness seized Christine that this was far worse than it looked. Will Kearny stood panting heavily, putting a split-knuckled hand to his bruised jaw as he took in that the battle was ended. But Mallison was totally soundless and untwitching. Christine rushed forward to his still form and dropped to her knees.

Tentatively, she touched him. Getting no

response, and feeling the coming-on of a sick dread, she bit her lip and put her hands on him, searching for a pulse, a heartbeat.

There was none.

'Oh, my God!' she said in a stricken voice. 'He's dead! You've killed him. *You've killed my father!*'

'Dead? Your father?' Kearny replied dumbly. 'What in Jesus's name are you talking about?'

She saw him through a blur of tears. 'My real name is Christine Mallison,' she jerked out. 'He didn't know it yet, but this saloon keeper was my father, whom I'd come to find after my estranged mother's death back East.'

As Kearny took in the meaning of the revelation she'd sprung on him, the shocked expression on his face turned to misery. 'Well, I'll be damned,' he said.

'Yes, you probably will be,' she said, with a catch in her voice. 'It's true what they say: you're a killer – and I hate you!'

He tried to lay his hands on her shaking shoulders as she straightened up.

'By all that's holy, that's no way to talk. You know I didn't mean this to happen,' he said. 'Mallison was a misguided man, maybe wickedly so, but he didn't deserve to die.'

She shook free from his restraining hold and flung herself sobbing across the cot. 'Oh, how senseless this all is! I thought you were strong and kind and gentle. I thought – I thought I was falling in love with you. How can I now?'

'I've lost you then,' Kearny said, a flintiness in his tone.

In her desolation, she was amazed he could be so obtuse. 'I hadn't seen my father since I was a ten-year-old kid in pigtails, but he was my only blood relation in the world. And you're the one who's killed him! I'd never be able to turn my back on that. Get away from here, you fool!'

'But why? You'll need someone–'

'Not you! They'll come and find you, and this time they'll hang you for murder!' she railed passionately. 'It'll be too much. I can't stand more blood and death. Leave me! Go quickly before they look for you!'

'I'm surprised you can care about that part,' he said, looking like he'd been kicked in the belly. Then he turned away and left her without looking back. She heard his footsteps clump across the landing and pad down the carpeted stairs.

She believed she'd never see him again.

Will Kearny made himself scarce. But he couldn't bring himself to ride out of the country. Remembering Pete Thwaites's convenient hideout at the Navajo's Cave, he holed up there, keeping a sharp eye for the first signs of a manhunt come to rout him out.

None came. He had the place to himself, the scuttling lizards and the scolding jays. Sometimes a buzzard circled. Kearny got the idea the evil bird was studying on when he, Kearny, might become a menu item.

He had long, empty hours to mull his predicament and the fate of the girl who'd called herself 'Smith' but had revealed she was Mallison's lost and forgotten daughter. Bitterly, he savvied that his standing with Christine was now below zero.

Did it really matter anymore? The pity he felt for the girl was surely self-pity. Her innocence was no more than an air; a fiction on a page of his life now turned over. He couldn't flip it back and change the print. Christine Mallison was scarcely untutored in the sordid side of life. God, he knew that! Not through being naïve had she made her damnable choices.

But some nights, as he tossed in his blankets, he thought he would go mad imagining her with various randy cowpokes in the tawdrily refurbished room above the saloon in Rawhide Fork.

Christine fell short of beautiful in the regular sense, being beanpole slender. Yet with her mop of brushed-out hair, her even though slightly angular features and hauntingly saddened eyes, she was beautiful to him.

When he did sleep, he'd see her in his nightmares without her clothes, like she'd been when he'd rescued her from Finnegan's cabin, but in her room at the Pleasure Palace.

He hoped her courage would see her through till – what?

He groaned in despair and dropped his head into his hands. Way back in Santa Fe, he should've forced her to return to New York City, where she could have aspired to return to the genteel circles of her deceased mother's set; her own kind of people. But when he'd told her she wouldn't like this rough country, she'd scorned his fears and hinted at the darker side of the Eastern cities and the hypocrisy of their civilized customs.

Kearny was absorbed in his self-recriminations over Christine when he was caught flatfooted early one morning. He was lighting the kindling sticks of his breakfast cook fire.

'Will Kearny!' a voice halloed from the brushy stream bed. 'Easy now! This is a friendly visit.'

'Pete Thwaites!' Kearny exclaimed bemusedly. 'Thank God you weren't no scalp hunter.'

The old rancher emerged into view from the gloom of the thickets and came on foot up to the camp. He let his eyes rove from the fire to the cave. He scowled at Kearny. 'The gossip up-trail was yuh gone on the dodge straight after Mallison's death an' I been wonderin' if I'd find yuh up here. I picketed the black in the meadow an' pushed on careful.'

'It's good to see you, Pete. But what on earth are you doing, coming back to these parts?'

'Unfinished business, yuh might say. I came lickety-split after I stumbled on the truth 'bout Rawhide Fork in a barroom in Santa Fe.'

'The truth...' Kearny echoed hollowly. 'What truth?'

'The truth that Franz Sturman is back of a snake-slippery piece o' crooked work, sure 'nough.'

Kearny wagged his head, side to side. 'You're talking in riddles, Pete. What've you got on Sturman?'

'Don't ride me, ol' pard. I'm a-tryin' to tell yuh, ain't I? It's a kinda complicated story.'

Thwaites rubbed his whiskered jaw. 'I got to drinkin' in the capital with a coupla them thar railroad survey fellers, workin' fer a sanctimonious jasper name o' Hiram Halliday.'

Kearny nodded. 'I've heard of the man myself. Owns hotels, too. A pillar of church-going society, they do tell.'

'Yeah, waal lissen, will yuh? When they heerd I was from this country, these survey fellers tol' me a lawyer man had bin to see boss Halliday an' persuaded him to re-route the spur line that was s'pposed to run to sidin's an' loadin' pens at Rawhide Fork. They got new orders to put in their pegs aimin' fer Jamesville.'

'That one-horse Mex burg!' Kearny exclaimed. 'What the hell for?'

"Cause the infamy o' railhead towns is a sore point with Mr Godly Halliday. His Bible-bashin' pals look down their noses at the drifters, gamblers and speculators they congregates. Halliday is mighty sensitive about it. The lawyer was that rat Seabury Reece an' he tol' Halliday Rawhide Fork was

225

a Babylon o' the frontier, full o' owlhoot trash, drunkenness, gamblin' an' lewd women. Whereas Jamesville still had a mission, a school taught by convent nuns an' all.'

Kearny's eyes suddenly blazed with dawning understanding and anger. He recalled discussing with the barber in Santa Fe the pockets of Spanish feudalism that persisted in the territory and the stability endowed by the old aristocratic families with their traditional religious values.

'By God, I begin to see purpose to what Sturman and Reece have been up to – from getting rid of Marshal Gurney onward. They want Halliday's railroad to bypass Rawhide Fork. But how does that profit them?'

By way of answer, Thwaites picked up a stick and scratched a map in the powdery grey ashes beside the firepit.

'When he's got the Rockin' T sewed up, Sturman's holdin's'll straddle the entire valley. The rails've gotta get through it someplace to make Jamesville.'

Kearny kept a rein on his patience, watching Thwaites append initials to his sketch at key points – RF and J; A and RT. He whistled softly.

'I see what you mean,' he said.

226

Thwaites smiled crookedly and made a final jab with his stick. 'An' thar ain't no way 'round the pass at the top end o' Rockin' T. Sturman figgers he'll hold the whip hand. He can name his own price fer puttin' his signature on a paper givin' Halliday's railroad comp'ny a right o' way.'

Kearny felt bitterness he could taste at how Sturman had fooled them.

'We've got to stop him, but how?' he said. 'The fancy tale Reece has told Halliday is about true. The town's gone all to hell. Folks won't hear us out. Mayor Martinez is plumb blind to how they've been bamboozled and is glad to heap blame on those he sees as individual troublemakers, including myself. We're just two men against the might of Arrowhead's hired gunnies and a whole town.'

Thwaites took out his corncob and tobacco and packed fragrant golden flakes into the pipe's blackened bowl. He was undeterred by the acid in Kearny's tone.

'Reece is the weak spot in Sturman's armour,' he said. 'He gits back to Rawhide Fork by scheduled stage today. Now we know the game, two of us is more 'nough to grab the sonofabitch an' git him to spill the beans to Martinez an' his crowd on how

Sturman plotted to destroy the town's respectability an' future; how folks was duped inta payin' fer the "brides". Once we got the town council sidin' us, we can hustle up a posse an' tackle Sturman an' Arrowhead with even numbers.'

'Forcing Reece to confess is a good plan of action,' Kearny said. 'But Rawhide Fork is Arrowhead's town now. With the likes of Bull Jusserand and Sturman's other hard-cases loitering around, Reece will stand his ground and holler for help the minute anyone accosts him. And I ain't hankering to show up in a town where they've a rope necktie waiting me.'

'Yuh gotten a good brain-box, Will,' Thwaites acknowledged with a sage nod. 'How say we meet the stage afore it gits to town, at Borge's relay station? With what I already got to tell 'em, I can prob'ly fix a gab-fest with Martinez an' the council at the abandoned Rockin' T layout, haulin' Reece along thar.'

Kearny was impressed with the scheme's possibilities, except for the one unanswered snag that remained.

'But the town still ain't going to swing in behind us. Not after I struck Seth Mallison dead. We won't get near a hearing. Fact is, they'll be liable to string me up long before we can get Reece to confess anything.'

'Thet ain't necessarily so,' Thwaites said mysteriously, firing up his pipe. 'Yuh ain't hist'ry yet, Will. It hinges on somethin' I larned way back. Jest give me the mornin' to check it out, will yuh? Then we can lick this thing.'

16

SHOWDOWN AT ARROWHEAD

The death of Seth Mallison that was such a seemingly fatal blow to the hopes and prospects of Will Kearny didn't sit ideally with Franz Sturman either. When Baldy Hogsden relayed to the range hog the startling news that Mallison had a long-lost daughter now in residence at the saloon, he considered it a messy complication.

He poured some whiskey from a cut-glass decanter into a heavy-based tumbler and went and stood legs apart before the massive stone fireplace in his parlour at the Arrowhead ranch house. He threw back his head, reviewing his options, then he spoke.

'It galls me some, but it won't matter much more than a pinch of goat shit,' he said. 'Reece will fix it pronto when he gets back from Santa Fe. Meantime, the Pleasure Palace must keep operating no matter what. If Mallison had died intestate, without blood kin, the property would've

231

gone by law to the Territory of New Mexico. In due course the Territory would've sold it to the highest bidder, and since I already hold a mortgage against half the value of the dump, that would've been me.'

Hogsden paused in chewing his wad with a perplexed grunt. 'So what do we need do, boss?'

'Observe the proprieties. This young woman ain't going to be bruised up for long over a pa she ain't seen in years. You'll take her my condolences and an invitation to visit with me – a quiet vacation at Arrow-head away from the scene of her father's death till the dust settles.' Sturman swirled what was left of the whiskey in the bottom of his glass before tossing it off. 'Since she's cat-house bait, she's plainly the type that knows what side her bread's buttered. We'll reach an accommodation.'

Hogsden's frowning face slackened in a brown-stained grin. 'I seen the filly, boss. An accommodation, huh? The boys'll envy yuh the chance.'

'That so?' Sturman drawled, a spare answering smile breaking over his square face. 'Maybe I'll give her the chance to prac-tise her female arts, if'n she ain't too raddled.'

232

The blistering sun was starting to wester in a brassy sky when Pete Thwaites returned to the Navajo's Cave. He brought back with him on a lead rein a docile saddled gelding, hired from a livery barn.

'What did you find out?' Keamny asked him eagerly.

Thwaites mopped the sweat from his brow and pulled out his watch from a vest pocket to see that it was five minutes short of two o'clock. 'Never mind fer now,' he rasped. 'We ain't got time to lose. Mebbe we'll talk about it on the way out to Borge's stage station.'

But by the time they'd ridden Indian file down the narrow stream bed to the prairie, with the exchange of no more than the odd word possible, the pressure was on to make their planned rendezvous with the incoming stagecoach from Santa Fe. They kicked their mounts into a gallop, conversation out of the question.

Borge's relay station was a cluster of adobes and corrals seventeen miles up the ungraded roadway from Rawhide Fork. Borge was long dead and gone, but an old Mexican and his wife were on hand to tend and hitch the stage teams and provide refreshment and a place of brief rest for passengers.

Kearny and Thwaites had only just tied their horses in a scrap of weed-grown shade around a trough behind the main structure when the stage rolled in. It arrived in the yard out front with the blowing snorts of the tired team, a jingle of harness metal and a creak of leather thoroughbraces.

They heard the good-natured cussing and pleasantries the stage driver exchanged with the Mexican as he swung down from the box, and the groans as passengers clambered out to ease cramped limbs and aching joints.

By pre-arranged plan, Thwaites went to seek out the lawyer booked to be riding the stage. Kearny listened, ears straining.

'I come lookin' fer yuh, Reece.'

'Thwaites! What do you want, man? And when are you going to sign those Rocking T deed papers?'

'Step aroun' the back, will yuh? Where we can talk private.'

'Well, you must have something on your mind,' Reece said gruffly. 'Meeting me like this. I'll give you a moment, but no more, understand.' When Seabury Reece saw Kearny, he pulled up with a stiff jerk, suddenly realizing things might be headed horribly wrong for him. 'Kearny, too! What is all this?'

'The jig's up, Reece,' Kearny announced with grim satisfaction at the lawyer's nervousness. 'We know about the guff you've been feeding Hiram Halliday in Santa Fe, and why. Your stage trip ends here. We've brought you a mount and you'll tell the stage driver you're riding with us.'

'I think not!' Reece blustered, his face gone sickly pale under a sheen of sweat.

Kearny drew his Colt and levelled it, his thumb on the smooth hammer.

He cocked the heavy gun with an ominous click. 'You'll do like we say.' And he nodded his head at the saddled livery bronc. 'We don't want to pack you out of here roped across that hull, but if we have to, it'd be a damned pleasant chore.'

True to his toady type, Reece was a coward. He went along quietly. In fact, he was so meek, Thwaites was finally able to explain to Kearny how he knew his ex-foreman was in no danger of citizens' arrest.

'It all came out at Seth Mallison's inquest, Will. He didn't die from no punch o' your'n. Like I suspicioned, the coroner ruled his ticker gave up on him. Angina. I got the final facts this mornin', but I knowed a long time Mallison had gotten hisself heart troubles.'

Kearny felt his own heart leap against his ribs. It beat faster with strange excitement and his fist clenched the chestnut's reins into a knot. 'Why did no one tell me?' he asked stupidly.

'They should've oughta wised you up, I guess, but you'd lit a shuck kinda sudden, long afore it was announced in public at the hearin'.'

Kearny, though mightily relieved, was baffled yet. 'You say you knew before this morning about Mallison's weak heart. How so?'

'It were Doc Oram. He ain't never heerd o' thet patient confiden – confi–' The old man stumbled over the long word he was trying to complete. 'Hell, yuh know what I means: confiwhatsit. Fer a sawbones, he was always a godawful blabbermouth. Specially when yuh got him sharin' a jug.'

For Kearny, it was like playing thimblerig – but with the surprise of a winning pea under each cup as it was turned. Thwaites's revelations fitted in with what he himself knew about Oram, though being a healthy young man and a cowpuncher who didn't crowd his luck when doing risky tasks, he'd never had personal call on the town doctor's services.

His growing elation had plenty to do with being square with the people of Rawhide Fork. It had even more to do with a blossoming hope that he might now be able to salvage his stock with Christine Smith.

A half-hour's ride brought them onto what had been Rocking T graze.

Then they were above the home lot where the grass gave way to the clump of cedars and a faint updraught carried the scent from sagebrush downslope.

True to their promise to Thwaites, Ramon Martinez and his cronies had assembled. Horses and rigs – buggies, surreys and buckboards, most of them shabby – stood in the yard, and someone had opened up the old, double-doored barn. A ragged cheer greeted the trio's arrival.

Not only council committeemen had come. Word had been whispered around the towners and the small ranchers who'd mustered the several hundred dollars needed to finance the ill-fated brides scheme. Since the character of the women had become known, they'd been hard put to suppress their feelings. With fresh information on who'd fooled whom, they were raring to redirect their anger from a fiddlefooted ex-range-boss to a shyster lawyer.

Martinez, as chairman, called the packed meeting to order and welcomed the audience. 'And let me extend an even warmer, not to say hot, welcome to our guest of honour, Mr Seabury Reece, directly back from Santa Fe. Mr Reece is here to answer questions and confirm in person rumours you'll no doubt have heard....'

Intimidated by their numbers, Reece sang.

Temperance Doe was working the main room at the Pleasure Palace with the help of the pudgy barkeeper. Business was slow. The few customers in the flashy new surroundings included Doc Oram and Bull Jusserand.

As she passed by the Arrowhead hulk's table, she saw a glint in his gaze light up the swarthy face that always seemed so conscienceless and cruel. He took in the smooth roll of her ample hips.

'Some eyeful, ain't she?' he observed to Oram. 'Hey, madam! There ain't no one else here needin' it. What say we go upstairs, cheap rates?'

The idea repulsed Temperance despite her broad tolerance. Any girl going with Jusserand deserved double rates. His habits and person were unclean. And he was so bone-crushingly big. You had your work cut out thinking up ways to stop him from going on top. 'Haven't you got something else you should be doing?' she asked.

Jusserand blinked slow-wittedly. 'Naw. I was to've brung lawyer Reece out to Arrow-head when he got in on the afternoon stage, but he weren't.'

Doc Oram chuckled over his whiskey. 'Of course not. Mr Reece was met at Borge's and hustled off to the meeting.'

'Meeting? What yuh talkin' about, Doc?'

'The meeting where Mr Reece's going to be made to tell tales by Pete Thwaites and Will Kearny. Haven't you heard? The knowledgeable betting is for danders being raised and a big deputation afterwards, out to your boss's layout. I figure that less it's kept a surprise, there'll be big trouble – a gunfighting showdown maybe, and more than a few *hombres* for me to patch up.'

Temperance had learned that the frail physician with the octagonal, silver-rimmed glasses and a liking for whiskey had been Rawhide Fork's medico since he'd come here after the War, in which he'd served as a surgeon for the Union. She'd also noted that hard liquor (which he called wild mare's milk) had a powerful loosening effect on his tongue and that he was a goldmine of information.

His latest nugget brought her up with a start.

It also affected Jusserand. His brows knitted and he cuffed back the coarse black hair he'd let tumble across his low forehead.

'Trouble? At Arrowhead? Why the hell didn't yuh say so sooner, yuh ol' stumble-bum? I gotta tell the boss pronto. Ain't no one facin' down the brand an' not goin' up ag'inst me!'

He gulped his mug empty and pushed up off his chair so quickly its legs tangled with his own. He kicked it away and rushed out, his stomping footfalls rattling glassware and glitzy fittings.

Temperance turned on Doc Oram, assailed by anxiety and guilt that made her mouth and throat go dry. 'Now look what you've done!'

'Never mind, my dear,' Oram defended himself. 'Busted chair legs mend faster than men's.'

'You fool! I didn't mean the chair. It's Chrissie ... Seth Mallison's daughter. I advised her it was safe to go visit at Arrowhead. To stop Sturman from foreclosing on this deadfall. She's no dewy-eyed virgin an'll do what's needed, but she'll stand to die in a gunfight!'

The meeting in the Rocking T barn was close to unanimous. Franz Sturman had a gall – always had – but this time was the time to call him out, gunfighting crew or no.

'How else do we get to an end to it?' asked one rancher. 'We never showed any guts before an' look how it's landed us. I say we gotta do somethin' while we got a chance.'

'Surprise will put the odds in our favour,' agreed Ramon Martinez.

'Well, I guess I'm game enough if everybody else is,' said one of the soberest towners.

'We brought our arms, didn't we?' added a hothead. 'By Christ, I'm good 'n' ready!'

'We need a leader,' said Mayor Martinez. 'I propose we reinstate the post of marshal immediately and I nominate Will Kearny.'

Pete Thwaites bobbed up. 'I second thet! Then we can do this lawful-like.'

The vote was completed by a show of hands. Kearny accepted, though he was a mite leery, since he felt he'd somehow been backed into a corner.

'A dubious honour this,' he muttered to Pete. Peace officers were obliged to maintain the respect awarded them. That often involved the quick draw of a gun. Though Kearny had no doubt of his ability, he knew a reputation made with a gun died with a gun.

With the hint of oncoming dusk in lengthening shadows, fifteen riders climbed into their saddles and pounded off across the range in a ragged column for the Arrowhead spread.

Short of an hour later, the impromptu posse reached Sturman's red-roofed *hacienda* set in its lush valley. It was confounded to be met outside the yard by a small group headed up by Louey Jusserand and Baldy Hogsden.

Jusserand stood four-square in their path, pointing a menacing Winchester .44. The other men, Kearny saw, were Arrowhead's lately-hired gunnies rather than genuine ranch-hands. The posse was expected.

Hogsden yelled, 'That's fur 'nough. Tell yuh boys to turn aroun' an' ride, Martinez!'

Kearny cursed. 'They've gotten wind somehow.'

Martinez said, 'Lower that gun, Jusserand. Marshal Kearny is here to arrest you on suspicion of the murder of Arch Leggat. We're taking you to the Rawhide Fork lock-up. Likewise your boss, Franz Sturman. Warrants have been sworn out on charges of fraud and as an accessory to murder, and we aim to serve them.'

'Yuh'll never make 'em stick,' Hogsden jeered.

'We'll let the circuit judge decide that, Hogsden. Put down that weapon, Jusserand, and let us by.'

Glowering like a surly child, Jusserand caught up with the import of the message. 'I says not!' he roared. 'Scatter to hell an' gone, yuh no-account bums!'

He worked the lever of the Winchester. Hogsden screeched, 'There's too many witnesses – not now, yuh idiot,' and jogged his arm as he triggered.

The shot went over the posse's heads. The crash of the report reverberated across the range and was flung back as an echo by the walls of the ranch buildings.

Some of the towners' horses, being gun-shy, were startled into prances and whin-nies. Kearny saw the line backing him break up. 'Hunt cover and unhorse!' he cried, fearing an exchange of gunfire at this stage would end in a bloody rout.

The possemen broke up, swinging their lathered mounts round and plunging off the trail to the yard and into the trees that lined it.

Luckily, their confusion was matched by their opponents'.

Jusserand grunted belly-deep. 'Yuh made me miss, Baldy!' In mindless petulance, he reversed the smoking Winchester in his huge hands and swung it from the muzzle end. The stock, describing a long, sweeping arc, smashed heavily into the side of Hogsden's skull.

Hogsden gave a strangled cry and went down like a floppy doll. From the twist of his neck and the disposition of his arms and legs, Kearny knew he wouldn't ever be spitting tobacco juice again.

Several regular 'punchers and the Arrowhead *cocenero* came out of the long, low bunkhouse and raced to a corral where a remuda of cow ponies stomped their hoofs restively. They began saddling up.

'Let 'em ride,' Kearny instructed the men siding him. 'It's not them we want.'

Jusserand and Sturman's mercenaries retreated to the ranch house, knowing hell could open for them any moment in the dust of the open yard. Hogsden's body was left to lie. Doors slammed behind them and Kearny noticed all the windows were shuttered.

After the Arrowhead riding crew had ridden out, a thick silence descended. In the gathering dusk, Kearny assessed the situation. To fire on the thick-walled *hacienda* demanding surrender would be a waste of lead. To leave the cover of the trees to cross the bare stretch of ground to the house would be foolhardy. This was stalemate.

Kearny looked at the sky through aspen leaves, frowning grimly. The sun was well down. Once it went below the horizon, night would fall quickly. Under the cover of darkness, anything might happen. The cornered lobos could even break out and Sturman get away from them yet.

He was not alone in his thoughts. An informal council of war got under way. Blood was fired up; the appetite for revenge sharp. One of the more adventurous hotheads said, 'Let's smoke 'em out. We'll roll a fire wagon across the yard an' let it crash inta the gallery. It's timber an' so's the doors and shutters. It's been a long dry summer, pards.'

The suggestion was met with a growling chorus of approval. Kearny had reservations, a nervous foreboding, but with no alternative to offer, he didn't try to over-rule the idea. 'Could be something rash and impulsive is called for,' he thought aloud.

Three of the possemen worked round the yard's perimeter, avoiding sight lines from the ranch house and fossicking through the empty barns and stables. They found what they wanted: an old Conestoga and a store of filled barrels of coal oil.

Hands eager to end the standoff quickly manhandled the wagon into place on the trail. The barrels were loaded into its long, deep bed. The discoloured Osnaburg cloth stretched over its bentwood bows was then saturated with the reeking oil.

A team of eight straining men, using the wagon body as their cover, put all their weight into setting it trundling toward the house on its wide, iron-rimmed wheels. Rusted axles creaked in the forged fixtures of the running gear's mountings.

'She's goin'! Let 'er rip!'

There was a fusillade of shots from the house as the pushers scattered and another man tossed a flaming brand into the moving wagon. In seconds, the Conestoga, blazing fiercely, smashed into the gallery, toppling support posts.

What with the noise and the oily black smoke and his attention riveted on the house, Kearny didn't notice the approaching dust banner till the spring buggy that churned it up wheeled into the yard.

Kearny recognized the buggy and the old plug of a hammerheaded grey between its shafts. They belonged to Doc Oram, who was himself driving the conveyance, hauling up on the leather ribbons bunched in his hands. Sat beside him was Temperance Doe.

Before the buggy had jolted to a halt on its springs, Temperance was jumping down, skirts held high. Kearny rushed out to meet her, risking slugs fired blindly through the smoke from the house. He waved his arms.

'Get out of here, the pair of you! Hell's a-popping!'

Temperance was greatly agitated by the bedlam around her. 'Will!' she exclaimed. 'Chrissie's in there!'

The blood in Kearny's veins went to icy slush. 'What did you say?'

Temperance repeated it, adding explanatory details he didn't bother to hear.

'No one fire on the house!' he yelled. 'I'm going in!'

'Are you crazy, Kearny?' said Martinez. 'Look at the smoke! Every sonofabitch in there is coming out real soon, and they'll hoist their hands as our prisoners or get cut down.'

But Kearny didn't fancy the chances that this might save Christine Smith. What if Sturman and his shootists came out guns blazing? A stray bullet in a crossfire and Christine would be dead. On the other hand, Sturman might choose to stay put and die of smothering by smoke, forcing Christine to share his fate.

When he pounded across the baked grit of the yard, Pete Thwaites was at his heels to back him up. Kearny said, 'We'll smash in a window shutter upwind of the smoke.' He stooped to grab hold of a fallen gallery post.

The makeshift battering-ram splintered wood and glass at their third thrust. A wild volley of gunfire poured from the aperture, tearing a hunk from Kearny's hat brim.

Thwaites backed off, picked up his Sharps .50–90 from where he'd put it down, and fired into the shadowy interior. The buffalo gun wasn't made for close work, but its thunderclap boom and a chilling scream from one of the defenders effectively per-suaded them to retreat to other rooms, slamming doors behind them.

Kearny vaulted the window-sill, went across the room at a crouching run, kicked open the door, and instantly cut loose with his Colt into the smoky dimness beyond.

'Give yourselves up and you'll be spared!' Kearny shouted. He was in a passage, and he emptied his Colt at random, firing through shut doors above head height, before prising new cartridges from the loops of his belt and recharging the six-shooter in all chambers.

His daring paid off. The hardcases were trapped. Not knowing the scale of the unexpected assault, cornered in parts of the *hacienda* filled with the choking fumes of burning oil, they began flinging open all exits. Because of Kearny's order, no one was firing on the house from outside anymore.

Sturman's hired trash saw it as preferable to chuck out their guns and follow them, empty hands raised, yelling surrender.

Kearny and Thwaites checked several rooms, only to find them abandoned. The smoke was wafting into the house and in one room furnishings were afire. From an open window, Kearny saw Temperance. 'Have Christine or Sturman come out?' he called anxiously.

She told him no, and he groaned.

Thwaites said, 'Thar's still Sturman's study.'

The door was closed against them, but Kearny wrecked the lock with a .45 slug and they crashed it open.

Christine Smith cringed against a far wall. Her drawn face was marble-pale; her pupils dilated in a violet-blue gaze of horror. Sturman was behind the desk, stuffing papers which weren't stockmen's journals into a satchel. Bull Jusserand, his loyal dog, was at his side, hefting a Smith & Wesson revolver.

For the bat of an eyelid, the tableau held, then with a blistering curse, Jusserand came out of his frozen stance and let the revolver's hammer fall.

'I kill him, boss!'

Twisting, Kearny felt the heavy slug rip through his vest and sear his chest and side. It spun him halfway round and his feet went out from under him. He let go of his Colt involuntarily as he spread his hands to break his fall. The gun skittered across the varnished floor.

Simultaneously, Thwaites's buffalo gun exploded over his head and Jusserand was hurled backwards into a solid adobe wall decorated with a large map of middle and western America showing major drovers' trails.

Jusserand's head was blown apart like a

burst melon. His twitching body slid down the wall, and dragged down the map which flopped over him, a convenient shroud covering the grisly sight of his shattered skull.

Before Thwaites could fire again, Sturman had dropped the stuffed satchel and had himself got iron in his fist. He fired wildly without pause to aim, but managed to hit Thwaites in the right shoulder, which paralysed his gun arm, forcing him to back out of the room.

Sturman snarled gleefully. He strode round the mahogany desk onto the bear-hide rug, raised his revolver and pointed it point-blank at Kearny's head.

Kearny scrambled to get to his feet. Blood was soaking his shirt from his creased side. He made a desperate lunge toward his dropped Colt. He knew, though, that it was too late and he was a dead man. All Sturman had to do was pull the trigger.

It was then that Christine, silent and faint-looking, came to life with a choked cry. She rushed forward and stooped to grip the edge of the grizzly bear hide with both hands. She tugged with a might no one could have guessed she possessed.

When Sturman fired, the rug under his

feet was sliding back and he was off balance, starting to fall. His bullet went straight down, drilling a clean black hole through the shiny floorboards a split-second before his face smacked into them.

Kearny had all the reprieve he needed. He was dizzy and weak from blood loss, but what he had to do was clear and easy. He scooped up his Colt and laid it over Sturman's head.

Immediately after, Christine threw herself sobbing into his arms. Her slender arms swept around his neck and she kissed him.

They both – in the emotional, stress-releasing moment – understood everything.

In the following days, Pete Thwaites announced his retirement from active ranching – 'I'm puttin' myself out to pasture' – and gave his ex-ramrod a fifty-fifty partnership in the Rocking T. Will Kearny and Christine quickly announced their engagement. They planned to live on the Rocking T, and the doors of the Pleasure Palace had already been closed for the last time.

Temperance Doe and her co-workers boarded a stage for Santa Fe, their tickets paid for out of the Pleasure Palace's final balance on Christine's say-so.

Will Kearny and Christine were on hand to wave goodbye. He had his arm round her waist and she had a flushed brightness in her face. 'Now there stands a fine feller an' a fine woman, too,' said Temperance, sighing as the Concord rumbled away from the depot. 'The two of 'em go good together. A lot happened to her for sure, but she kept her soul intact. Look at her now: pretty as a picture, proud as a queen.'

'Thought you had designs on Kearny your own self,' said Black-eyed Sadie, sitting across from her in the swaying coach.

'I did for a fact, but you can't spoil a passionate romance, can you?' Temperance said practically. 'I mean nothing to him one way or the other.'

Sadie thought a cloudy wistfulness lingered in Temperance's eyes and that she was only saying these things to console herself and because it wasn't in her nature to keep a complete silence. Life was tough; life was sad. But sometime, someplace, for some folks the sun shone.

'Well,' Sadie said after a while, when she'd done thinking about it, 'I guess Rawhide Fork has gotten itself one bride.'

The publishers hope that this book has given you enjoyable reading. Large Print Books are especially designed to be as easy to see and hold as possible. If you wish a complete list of our books please ask at your local library or write directly to:

Dales Large Print Books
Magna House, Long Preston,
Skipton, North Yorkshire.
BD23 4ND